I0547820

Peter Fuller's Daughter

Susan Doyle

Peter Fuller's Daughter

Published by Sugilite Publishing, United Kingdom

ISBN: 978-1-7392827-6-9

CONTENTS

You may also enjoy Susan's other Books:

The Runt and the Ladybird.
ISBN 978-1-7392827-0-7
Publisher -- Sugilite Publishing
A reality-fantasy following the over-protected Conscience of
The Almighty, as she finally learns about the most important
thing in the whole World -- herself.

**The Nettle Wits --- The Legend of the Girl With No
Knickers**
ISBN 978-1-7392827-2-1
Publisher -- Sugilite Publishing
A delightful tale of leprechauns, climate change, and racism

The Cruel Land
ISBN 978-1-739287-4-5
Publisher -- Sugilite Publishing
The tale of a group, of mixed religion, as they struggle to
survive the East Pakistan War

PROLOG
I WONDER

Have you ever wondered what it's like to be dead? No? Then you've never been bashed with the bible.

I grew up with the bible, and it influenced my life, not with piousness, nor fundamentalistic views, nor Godliness of any sort, but with questions. So many questions. Don't get me wrong, I think religion is a powerful ally when the tribe needs to be held together, and a saviour when there is no other way out but the prayer, but it left me wondering what life was all about, and who was making the big decisions. If it was God who was making the decisions, then he's not always a nice God.

Now, I'd like to tell you the brief story of my life, a true story of a thirteen-year-old adult, a story which still leaves me wondering. So, do I ever wonder what it's like to be dead? Of course I do, don't we all?

So, before I tell you my story, take this little piece of advice: don't be in a hurry to find out what it's like! It'll come soon enough, hopefully later rather than sooner.

Peter Fuller's Daughter

CHAPTER 1
NOT A POPULAR MAN

The Maybush Estate, Blythburgh, Suffolk, England

Autumn 1844

Peter Fuller was not a popular man. He was the Estate Manager at the Maybush Estate, and was responsible for hiring and firing, organising work schedules, discipline, and gamekeeping. He took his work seriously!

He was also a layman preacher, based at the Bulcamp Workhouse, where his piousness was over-shadowed only by his intense enmity with the residents of the workhouse. 'You will reap what you sow!'

Peter Fuller was not a popular man.

Late November 1844

It was just beginning to get really cold when influenza hit the Maybush Estate. It was a virulent, spiteful strain of the disease, which respected nobody and swept through the estates like wild-fire, killing many and leaving communities in despair.

But, despite the plague, most of the families on the Maybush Estate found something to celebrate on the thirtieth of November 1844, when the very first victim was taken, when Peter Fuller went to meet his maker. He was not a popular man and most of the estate quietly rejoiced. However, the celebrations soon dwindled as more of the community were lost to the disease, and then, as quickly as it had come, the influenza left.

Back to normal? Not exactly, but life has to go on for the lucky ones.

Most of the people on the Maybush Estate that had been taken by the flu were children, with only two men being lost, one being the cowman, and the other my dad, Peter Fuller. I also lost my two youngest brothers, leaving just Mum, James and myself in the manager's house. Both the house and my life suddenly seemed very, very empty.

CHAPTER 2
A WONDERFUL GIFT

After the flu, December 1844

We were left reeling. I had recently turned thirteen, just at the age when you begin adult-life and you have to quickly learn about adult responsibilities, especially those related to the hardships of life. I sat at the window, wrapped in my shawl, watching a red squirrel dart up-and-down the bark, doing some mid-winter stocking up of his larder, and I wondered if we would ever again be as happy as him. But then I thought that he might well be putting on a brave face, after all, it was winter and he must have been having a hard one to be out at this time of year. He should have been fast asleep in his drey. However, I still wondered if we would ever again be as happy as him.

Don't get me wrong, my dad was never a bundle of fun, never made us laugh, spent his life indoctrinating us with his God, and ran my mum ragged at times, but he wasn't all bad. He kept us warm in the Manager's house, he fed us and clothed us, and I knew that we were so much more fortunate than most. Then there was his Bible. He made sure that we sat around the table every night while he read from the Bible, followed by some work on our numbers and our writing, but on Sundays we had a day off from it all, because we went to church. Sounds like more controlling behaviour from my dad, but not at all, in fact, by the time I was eight I could read, write and manage money, and stood head-and-shoulders above the other children who attended the school in Blythburgh. He had stopped us from attending the local school after I was seriously bullied by the poachers' sons, so he tutored us himself. He always said that education would see us through our lives, however long that may be. Then there were his secrets. We knew almost nothing of his life before Mum, except that he was a fist-fighter, and he made sure that his secret life remained secret. He's now dead, and those secrets have followed him to the grave. I'll never know who he really was.

As I sat watching through the window at the squirrel, I wondered if he could read and write. Perhaps his world was different to mine, so maybe he didn't need to read and write to be happy, but then I looked to Mum, who could read and write, but not very well. She never seemed very happy, just serious, sometimes a bit vacant, always working in the house and could never relax. I suppose it was understandable being married to a self-righteous control-freak like my dad, but it was her choice and he never let her down when it came to looking after her needs, apart from, of course, love and affection; she received very little. My dad gave us everything that we needed, apart from affection. I never really learned quite what it meant to be loved by a man. It was probably all about having babies, the propagation of God's children, at least that's the impression I got from Dad and his bible.

That was when I realised how my sorrow was purely down to the loss of my two brothers, *not* to the loss of my dad, but the niggling thoughts of how we would feed ourselves without his income forced me to miss him, not for his love, but for his material input into our lives. Eighteen forty-four was not a good year to be poor.

Once the funeral was over, Mum sat us around the table and explained that we were now starting out on the new journey through life, without Stephen, Alfred and my dad, and that we would be fine.

"But Mummy, I'm hungry." James, just eight years old with the whole World on his shoulders, sighed like an old man. "Now the chickens have gone, can we get some food from the store?"

But no, the store account was closed as soon as Dad died, as it was paid out of his wages, so without cash we could buy nothing, and the rest of the estate hated Dad so much that there was no charity coming our way. We were out of food and hungry, but Mum had an idea.

Part of Dad's work was that of gamekeeping, one of his responsibilities that Mum used to get involved with, and she would often accompany him on his rounds. She knew where every illegal snare and man-trap was set, so, she wrapped up and went into the dark, where she would search the snares and hopefully return with a rabbit. I put the latch on the door as she left, then waited with James, the oil lamp flickering and the small fire crackling as we cuddled to keep warm, James giggling at the thought of some fresh food, and me trying not to be too optimistic, then we heard something at the door.

Somebody pushed on the door, making the latch rattle, so we tensed up and waited for a knock, as Mum normally would have done. Nothing for a good few seconds.

"Might not be Mum," I whispered, and hung onto him.

Then the door knocked in Mum's fashion, and after a few seconds, Mum's voice asked to be let in.

James's face lit up as he rushed over, opened the door, and in fell our mum. She went straight down onto the stone floor, and whimpered, injured.

She had been hit hard in the face, her nose bleeding and right eye rapidly closing up, and James burst into tears. I helped him to get her up, into the chair in front of the fire, and without saying a word, she pointed at the kettle, so I took it from the fireplace, and used the warm water to bathe her face. Once the blood was off, I could see that it was a stick or club that had hit her face, not a fist but something which could have done some real damage.

The others really did hate us. What were we to do?

She never said a word, but her look of horror said it all. She was terrified and angry, a dangerous mix which would either lead to forgiveness or revenge, and if Dad was here, he would preach forgiveness, then practice revenge. I promised to remind myself, from time to time, that Dad had some *very* good points.

Then somebody else banged on the door!

"Stay there!" She jumped over to the table and took the rolling pin into her right hand, moved slowly to the door, and I grabbed the poker then stood behind her. "Who's there?" Nobody answered. "Who's there? Speak!" Still no answer.

I moved to the window and looked out into the dark of the night. After a couple of seconds my eyes adjusted, and I could see a small shape moving away from the house, then it melted into the night. I thought it was….. no, couldn't have been.

Then Mum shouted, "I coming out! What goes around, comes around! I'll crown you, you bastard!" She waited a couple of seconds then threw the door open, and leapt out, swinging her pin around her head and almost tripped ass-over-tit.

I rushed out to help her steady herself, then we both looked down at her foot, which was tangled in a sack, the sack which had been left on our door-step. I carefully moved to the lane, poker at the ready, but the dark figure had gone, so we moved back inside, taking the sack with us.

Guess what was in the sack. Two fat, juicy rabbits!

It was like a gift from God, the most beautiful thing I had ever known, just when we were at our lowest. Perhaps I had been a bit spoiled, wanting for nothing material, but suddenly the most basic part of life seemed the most important, and we celebrated. James's little face had never looked so radiant, unlike poor Mum's.

The two rabbits were good and plump, and fed us for almost two weeks, by which time it was coming up to Christmas Eve, when the towering hulk of the vicar called on us. He had been Dad's only friend, and so was keen to help us, if he was able, so he sat at the table with the three of us and held council. He spoke to me and Mum about our future on the Estate, especially as Dad was no longer working, and promised that he would speak to Lady Maybush immediately after Christmas, about work for her and me in the house. It gave us a tiny light of hope. He also left some bread, sprouts, potatoes and cauliflower, which we very much appreciated.

Then it was Christmas Day. We had already spoken about how this Christmas would be a quiet one, respectfully remembering our two brothers who had been lost to the flu, and I do believe that James understood, but what he struggled to comprehend was our sudden, dire poverty, going into the Christmas celebrations with almost no food, and none of the personal gifts which would normally be shared. The more he stressed over it all, the more I became upset. I was hungry, but James was more than that, and he was just beginning to realise what he had lost, and could not understand any of it. If Dad was still alive he would probably spout on about 'You reap what you sow,' and tell us to repent. I was beginning to realise why he was hated so much. However, to be fair on his memory, he would never have allowed us to get so hungry. Sorry Dad.

Anyway, it was Christmas morning, so we were compelled to go to the service in the Estate church, and an hour or so before the service the vicar's trap pulled up outside the house. Lady Maybush alighted. She was on the final leg of her Christmas rounds, bearing gifts!

"Food!" James jumped up and down at the window. Traditionally her Ladyship came round with chickens on Christmas morning, but we had all thought that the flu would put the kibosh on those niceties. We were wrong. I cuddled James at the window as her ladyship stood talking to Mummy behind the door, and we swooned as we dreamed of plucking, drawing and spitting the bird, the smell of the basting cow-fat tickling our noses with ecstasy. "Food!" Just for a moment our heads took us to heaven and back.

Then her ladyship went.

Mummy gently closed the door with a slight tremble, and turned to us. Her face twitched. She then laid her head back and cursed like we'd never heard her curse before, and held out the special Christmas gift that the Lord and Lady had so kindly given us. Our hearts sank, the dreams of sizzling fat and tender chicken breast dying as quickly as our ecstasy, then she threw it at the fire-place! It narrowly missed the open fire.

They had so kindly given us a framed portrait of his lordship. I cried.

CHAPTER 3
MERRY CHRISTMAS

It took a little while to get over the shock of having a framed portrait of his lordship for Christmas dinner, but we still thought it proper to go to the church for the service. It may take our minds off our hunger.

Before we left for the church, Mummy told me firmly, "Stand proud, and if you have to look, look them in the face. We've done nothing wrong." We dressed up in our warmest shawls, with hats, scarfs and gloves, and set off for the freezing Christmas-morning service.

We entered the small church proudly with Mum sporting her black eye and scabby nose, and James hanging tightly onto my coat, as all eyes were focused our way. Then I saw Cordelia's long nose. She was sitting with her mum and three sisters, so I popped along the pews to wish her a happy Christmas. She was my best, sorry only, friend.

I held onto her arm. "Thanks. I know it was you."

"Shhh. Please don't tell anyone. They'll bully me." She spoke quietly, below her breath, but her mum overheard, and smiled. Cordelia, still whispering, told me that they had heard their neighbour bragging about hitting my mum in the woods, so Mrs Brown sent Cordelia straight round with the rabbits, ashamed to be part of the demonisation of my family, just because my father had a terrible job of work to do, and now he's dead they should all respect him by leaving us alone. I felt a beautiful, warm feeling knowing that it wasn't the entire population who thought of us as evil shits, just most of them. "But I've got to be careful, else they'll bully me as soon as I go out."

She was the oldest daughter of Mr Brown, the cowman, who was the other adult taken by the flu, just him and my dad, but he was not like my dad, he was liked. So, Cordelia's family had received a lot of charity from the estate, including several rabbits from the poachers, two of which made it our way. I needed to keep that very secret for the sake of Cordelia.

After several minutes I thought it best for all if I was to return to my own family and leave Cordelia's out of it, so I whispered, "Love you. Happy Christmas." But before I could stand up, Cordelia stood and called along the pews, "Happy Christmas, Mrs Fuller and James." Then her mum also wished my mum happiness, and poisonous whispering spread through the congregation. Mummy returned the compliment with supreme grace by politely acknowledging the wishes and holding her head high for all to see her damaged face, and to feel her defiance. I was very proud of her, but I quietly prayed that Cordelia had not soured the estate's charity towards them.

I was not impressed with the vicar's sermon. His words were nice for my dad and brothers, along with Cordelia's dad and all the other children who were taken by the flu, but it was all the will of God. I had been drilled for my entire thirteen years of life with the will of God, coupled with 'You reap what you sow,' and all the other contradictory statements which seem to exist purely to confuse us all enough to not be able to question the 'will of God', so we believe it. It's the simplest way, but so, so confusing. Best not to think about it, just float along with the community of worshipers. I just know that the estate's cowman, a good, popular man who was not very religious, was taken, as was the estate's manager, a hated, pious bully who bashed the bible, blindly and devoutly. Two from the opposite ends of the spectrum, so why would God select those two? Like I say, best not to think about it.

Anyway, this story isn't about God, it's about me, and my family's struggle through life towards that great pie-in-the-sky, Heaven.

We left the church after the rather strained service and

felt the warmth of the winter sun. It was the middle of winter, but still it was so much warmer outside than in the church, and I again wondered why churches had to be so cold. It must be some form of punishment for our sins, but if that's the case, wouldn't it be helpful to be told what we've done wrong, then we could adjust our ways, not just endure the punishment. I was feeling so anti-everything as we sat down in front of our open fire, warming our Christmas spirits and toes, but our tummies still groaned.

Then, even before we had come round from our sacred exposure, the door was banging. Mummy picked up the rolling pin and I the poker, then she answered it, before inviting the caller in. It was Cordelia!

"Happy Christmas!" She bounced in, plonked herself down beside me to catch the warmth, then held out her gift for the family. "It's from all of us. We've got plenty at home, so I hope you enjoy it." Her smile was as wide as the ocean and her nose as long as the pier, but I suddenly saw my best friend's real beauty. "I can't stay long, as we're eating soon, but I'll come round tomorrow and we can talk about things." She grinned into my face. "We need a plan."

She went before we really had chance to thank her. Her gift was a small hessian sack, which held something wrapped up in cabbage leaves, and it was warm. James's eyes almost popped out as I unwrapped the food, which was a cooked cockerel, still hot and smelling of goose fat. That Christmas we ate the best meal we'd ever had. As I cuddled James I knew that we would make it through, whatever happens, and would be as happy as the red squirrel, and that was my promise to myself and James.

If I knew then what was in store for us all, I may not have been so confident, but faith isn't about the reality of life, it's about belief, and at that moment, warm and fed, I believed.

CHAPTER 4
WE NEED A PLAN

That was Christmas, eighteen forty-four. It had capped off a terrible six weeks for us and Cordelia's family, but was a catalyst for hope as we all looked forward to eighteen forty-five. We had very little in our lives, but I was determined to have hope, after all, we all hope for a happy future, even if we can see little evidence of the good times, so, hope is what I had in abundance and it spurred me on. I was almost bursting with expectation as I walked across the fields with Cordelia.

Her clothes were warm, woollen, greeny-beiges and browns, and very similar to mine, but mine were newer. They always were. However, it never seemed to bother her that my clothes were always newer and smarter than hers, advertising that I was better off than her, and I don't think it bothered me, but I always noticed. Perhaps it bothered me a little, deep down, and I had always thought that it was one of the reasons that the other people on the estate never liked us: jealousy. But, Cordelia, nor her family, seemed to worry about it. Maybe when my clothes get older and dirtier, due to not having a dad to buy new ones, the others would accept me. Maybe not. The important thing was that Cordelia and I were both the same, whatever our clothing, and we bounced along the muddy path as if the past bereavements had never even happened.

"I love it when you're like this, all keen and up for it." She giggled.

She held my arm as we walked through the grassland. I had never known another real friend, and she was the same; we were a couple of outcasts. I never went to the school in the town, partly because I was bullied due to being the Manager's daughter, but mainly because my dad objected to what they taught us (which was never very much, anyway) and so he taught us to read and write through the daily bible readings, and then made sure we could do maths. At thirteen I was head-and-shoulders above the other schoolchildren, academically speaking, and quite pretty, so I had a confident future, but Cordelia was different. She never went to school in the town because she was very badly bullied due to her massive nose, and since her mum and dad were limited with their own reading abilities, she never received any worthwhile schooling. She was not well educated, and not very pretty, but she had a lovely heart.

"So, what we gonna do? You got any ideas?" She raised her eyebrows. "Haven't got dads any more, so we need to find our own fortunes. Ideas. We need an idea before we get into Bythburgh. Come on!"

I pulled my shawl tighter over my shoulder. The wind was quite cold. "We could go somewhere else, where there's future. You know, my dad's vicar-friend told him that Suffolk is the most deprived part of the country for farmworkers and lots of people have gone to Australia to farm. Loads more have gone to the north, in the mills, but that doesn't sound nice. Australia sounds all right, though."

She breathed in deeply and frowned at the same time. "My Uncle's gone to get rich in the gold mines. I told you about him. We could go there. We could go and look for husbands in better places." The frown continued. "Uncle has gone to Bolivia to get rich, but I don't think he's happy. He's written a letter to my dad, which didn't get here until after Dad died. I've got it here." She looked sheepishly at me. "We can't read it very well, now Dad's gone. Will you read it to me, please?"

I was honoured to be asked, so, "I could read to all the family."

"If you can read it just to me, then I'll tell them what's in it. That'll be best." She clearly had reservations about the letter's content. "I can make out some of it, but don't want

16

to tell the others until I know for sure. Without Dad to read it…. Will you read it to me?" She took the letter from inside her smock and handed it to me.

"All right. Now, there's a date. It's written about four months ago. Dear Peter, I hope you are all well, and the cows are behaving themselves. I have had a terrible time here, and have to tell you that poor Mary has passed away. I do not want to go into too much detail, but the mine is so high in the mountains that it is cold all year, and the Indians said that it gets so cold when the winter comes that they all go down lower. It's like living in Hell. When we arrived the Company lent everybody money to get set up, but we have not found much gold so the loan never gets paid back and never will, and I think I will be here until I die, and join Mary. Poor Mary wanted to work with me in the mines, but the Indians all said that if a woman goes into the mine, the gold will disappear, so she had to work on the slag with the other women, and there was a slip and she fell with two others. Please tell Pam gently. And please tell Cordelia not to dream of coming here. It is no place for a human, let alone a young girl. She must dream of better things, not this. I might see you all again one day, God willing."

Her face was very emotionless, despite a tiny couple of tears appearing, so I gave her a hug. Mary was her mum's twin sister, and Cordelia now needed to be the man of the house and tell the family, but it went deeper than that. She had told me before, many times, about her dream to join her uncle in the search for gold, and become rich, so she'd lost so much in those few weeks; her dad, her auntie, and her dream. We had both lost so much, but I felt that I was better equipped to move forward, and I felt a duty to my close friend to help her, and I had a warm feeling in my heart, knowing that she needed me. I wouldn't let her down.

"I could still read the letter to your family. It might be the easiest way to tell them."

She shook her head. "Thanks, but Mum's expecting me

to just tell her what's in it. I'll do it when we're all quiet and the little ones have gone to bed." She was no different to the rest of us, accustomed to death, so, she shrugged her shoulders, breathed deeply, then stated, "Need another dream, now."

We both thought privately as we walked the rest of the field, as far as the town, but as soon as we reached the church we turned round to walk home. There was nothing in the town for us, apart from bullying, so we turned our noses up to the few people in the street, and wandered back into the fields. Don't know why we even walked there, except that we needed to walk somewhere, to get out of the houses and share some time together.

"I know!" She shook my arm. "You could get married and I'd be your maid. You'd find someone easily, with your pretty face, good child-bearing hips on account that your dad fed you so well, and you can read and write and count, so you could teach. And I could look after your every need." With a smug grin, her nose standing proud and her eyes almost laughing, "Well? Any better ideas?"

"Stupid." I gave her a soft slap around the head, before I suddenly began to think about it. "Well, not the worst idea you've had, but I'm only thirteen, and the vicar's asking in the house about work in there for me and Mum."

"No chance! Unless, of course, His Lordship fancies you, and you could keep him warm in the mornings. I heard he's like that, in fact my dad said never to go in the big house alone, because he likes really young girls, even me with my face like a cunt."

"Don't say that! Some cows've got really pretty backends."

I received a slap around the head.

She, almost whispering, "Serious though, you need to be careful if you get work in the house. He's a right one." Her skinny face screwed up at the thought, and her nose twitched. "But you could tell *anyone* that you're sixteen and they'd believe you. You could find a young man with some money and be loads better off than my uncle and auntie in their search for gold. You wouldn't die of cold, or fall down a mountain. Then I could look after you, forever."

She was making a lot of sense, but I wasn't really happy with her tone, not about me, but about herself. I'd never noticed that she was as ugly as she made herself out to be, and as I looked sideways into her warm eyes, all I saw was a loyal friend, one which seemed to have given up on herself regarding men and sex, but why? We were only thirteen, just starting out on sexual life, but she assumed that nobody would care for her, nor love her. All I could think of was that she had been wound up by the bullies enough to start to believe it.

"I think you're lovely. Don't keep putting yourself down."

"Oooh, Eunice, do you fancy me? We could get married, stuff the boys, and live in sin, as your dad would put it."

She was still making a lot of sense, a couple of spinsters. But we couldn't feed ourselves, not without a man, so, I slapped her around the head, then she slapped me back and we had a friendly grapple, probably for fun, but just maybe for more. Mating play? We instantly stopped and walked ahead in silence, hiding our blushes from each other, keeping our private thoughts private. I don't know about Cordelia, but I had never felt like that before, that twinge in my tummy and a desire which clouded my mind as well as my mental composure. Silently, we moved towards home, stepping around the damp, muddy patches and veering out to avoid the brambles which hung across our path, and my mind raced.

Then, "Have you ever played with a boy?" I asked quietly, and looked around the empty field and along the hedge, fearful that there could be somebody lurking who had seen us frolicking. "You know, like boy and girl play?" But she just went sulky and looked away from me. I had touched a nerve.

I hadn't played with a boy, had never had the opportunity, but I had felt on several occasions that Cordelia wanted to tell me something, but was afraid to, and it was always when we spoke about boys. We were both at that age where it was beginning to intrigue us, but were afraid of it, so I put it all down to puberty, and accepted that we both had a lot to learn about life. It would be easier for her to learn if she was to become a little less afraid of it.

Anyway, we walked the rest of the field, along the hedge, and arrived at her little house, nestled in amongst three barns. It was the first time I had noticed that it was only about half the size of our house, as were most of the other farmworkers' cottages, and Cordelia's family numbered herself, four younger brothers and sisters, her mum, and up until recently, her dad. They all slept in one bedroom. Then I looked further past her house and noted that the other four cottages were all the same size, and two of the families were even larger than Cordelia's, all in one bedroom. Was that why the others all disliked my family, Jealousy? Perhaps it wasn't just about Dad being an over-conscientious manager.

"Come in here before you go." She led me into the smaller of the three barns, which was a calving shed, but no cows were in there. "No babies at this time of year." She nervously sat down on a bucket and tapped the one beside her. "I need to tell you, in case you get work in the big house." She took hold of my arm. "You know I said that Dad said that old Maybush is a dirty old man…. He didn't say that. I said it." She spoke quietly, intimately. "Well, I'm not allowed in the house any more. Her Ladyship won't allow me in any more, because when I used to help Dad in with his logs, old Maybush caught me in the hallway, and put his hand up my frock, and touched me. I didn't know what to do, because he's our Lordship, so I let him. Anyway, Lady Maybush caught us and she blamed me for it all, so I can't ever go in the house again. Never. So, if you get work in the house, he'll do the same with you, 'specially as you're so pretty. Definitely."

That hit the spot. Me and Mum were both secretly hoping to get work in the house, just so that we can stay in our home, but it suddenly frightened me.

She continued, "If he does try to do things with you, hit him and scratch him, else Her Ladyship'll think it's all your fault and kick you out. She's boss in the house, he just pays for it all." Then, with a grin, "What we really need is that plan, oh pretty one. A rich man for you. Unless, of course, I can find a blind, rich man for me. Must be one, somewhere."

A good bit of advice from my only friend, which I took rapidly on-board.

Peter Fuller's Daughter

CHAPTER 5
A GOOD REASON TO KILL

Over the next few days I spoke with mum about our future. We were still short of food, but Cordelia and Dad's vicar-friend dropped bits off as often as they could, since the rest of the estate continued to despise us, and we both felt that things would only change if we could get some work in the house. When I told her about what happened to Cordelia, she was not at all surprised, and suggested, "Perhaps that's why they don't have children, the old gal is cold and barren, so he looks elsewhere." I nodded in agreement, but wasn't really sure what she meant by it.

It was the first time Mum had spoken to me like an equal, two grownups discussing ours and James's future, and we both agreed that we couldn't plan anything until we knew about our employment on the estate, so, we spent the next few days trying to worry about only the present. Food and warmth, that was what we concerned our minds with, the essentials in life. It was depressing being in a hole with so few ways out, but I watched the red squirrel venturing out into the cold, never giving up nor moaning, and I promised myself that I would never weaken in my resolve to survive and to protect James, so it was up to me to do or die. I spent quite a bit of time walking with Cordelia, discussing our futures, but we never seemed to come up with much of a plan. However, we both vowed never to give up.

It was a couple of weeks into the New Year when Lady Maybush turned up outside our house in her carriage, parked on the lane, then alighted. She was not accompanied by the coachman, but by Dad's vicar-friend. They both came to the front door.

Mum let them in, and we almost exploded with anxious

expectation, James hanging tightly onto my arm, and me in a cold sweat. Our future was about to be clarified. Visions flashed through my head of a dirty old Maybush touching me up as I walked past him, but believe-you-me, that's better than starving or freezing to death. There was hope.

Then I suddenly felt James's eyes burning into mine, delving deeply into my head as he wondered what was really happening. He was too young to understand the intricacies of our situation, but he could always understand my face, and as he studied, I began to panic. A feeling of deep despair set about me, a feeling of doom, of the black angel descending down upon us, then I felt James's face against mine and I calmed. I needed him as much as he needed me.

Lady Maybush, in her tweed shooting breeches and jacket, stood in front of the vicar and took a deep breath. I could imagine her holding her shotgun in her left hand, readying herself for the game, with her dog handler waiting in the wings, behind, to retrieve the kill. Her face was indifferent. My face was nervous.

"Mrs Fuller, it has been a few weeks now since the tragic loss of your husband and children, but life must go on, and so must the business of the Estate." She was cold, as if reading from an invisible script. "It is with great regret to have to tell you that we have engaged a new manager, and he will start work on Monday. He'll be moving into this manager's house tomorrow. The vicar will explain." She stood aside to give the vicar some space.

Mum almost fell to the ground, while I tensed up like a cornered weasel, and James read my face. He began to cry.

The vicar stood forward and held Mum's arm, then led her to the fireside chair.

"Sit down and relax. I've managed to sort out some things."

Mum and me both managed to take some deep breaths, and so calmed enough to be able to listen.

He stood over Mum, looking down on her, and he was a

big man. "I've been able to sort out accommodation for you all." He stopped, pulled over the old country chair, and sat, so as not to be overpowering. "It's not what you've been used to, but it will give you the chance to start again. Mrs Fuller, due to your long standing in the parish, you've been accepted into the Blything Workhouse."

The end of life!

"No. Never! I'd rather die in the *hedges and gutters* than go there!" Mum began panting in a panic-attack, so I jumped over to sooth her. James just stood, never taking his eyes off my face.

The vicar placed his hand on her shoulder. "Please listen to what I've arranged. The children, or at least James, would be in the children's wing. You'd hardly ever see him, and I don't know quite how he'll be if he grows up in there, and I can't accept that of Peter's son. So, if you'll accept the help of the parish by bettering yourself in the workhouse, then I have a family that will take on Eunice and James." After a sigh, "It'd be the best for the two children. Please accept the charity."

Mum took some deep breaths before asking, "Why?"

"Peter, as much as he was disliked for his work, was a life-long friend of mine, as you know. I owe him some charity. Now, another friend of mine, one which Peter also was friendly with, lives on the outskirts of Yarmouth, and has a parish, and a vicarage which is big enough to take Eunice and James, and Eunice can earn her keep by helping to look after James and the other three waifs which they've taken in. It could be a new start for the children, especially as Eunice can give the younger ones regular tuition, alongside helping in the house. Not all children get that sort of break." He breathed deeply. "It's the best I could arrange for the two children, but it has to be your decision."

Mum eventually agreed to take the debatable offer of the workhouse, and gave the vicar permission to take me and James to Yarmouth. I quietly shuddered, as Mum sobbed.

It was arranged for the vicar to collect us all at the break of light next morning, but before they went, her Ladyship spoke.

She looked straight at me. "Don't waste your time going to Cordelia's, it's too late for goodbyes. We've also engaged a new cowman, so, Cordelia's family have already been delivered to the workhouse."

That was the final straw! I saw red, swung at the heartless bitch, but can't really remember if I managed to hit her, before the vicar grabbed me. I cried hysterically in his arms.

We spent most of the night crying as a family, with Mum refusing to even discuss the eviction, nor her pending internment, nor Cordelia's incarceration, nor the break-down of our family. She just said that there was nothing she could do about it, and it would be for the best, so don't even talk about it.

I have to admit, talking was not on my mind, either, but murder was. I just hoped that I had got the bitch a good one on the chin, but couldn't remember enough to get any satisfaction from it, and Mum's mind was numb at the time. It had been the culmination of years of loyal service from our two families, and, in the end, our kind never meant a thing to the likes of the Maybushes, unless they could use us. We were disposables. We were the poor.

"I think I'm going to kill her." I spoke quietly, so that James never heard. "She'll pay for what she's done to us and Cordelia. I'll make it my life-long quest."

Mum just shook her head.

CHAPTER 6
THE SHERRIFF'S NEPHEW

We were collected by the vicar just as the winter sun rose. It was freezing, and his trap was open, so the long journey to Yarmouth, by way of the workhouse, would be torturous. Mum made us go back inside and take some extra blankets to wrap ourselves in, but Her Ladyship's coachman stood in our way as we came out from the front door.

"They belong to the house!"

Suddenly the vicar stood over him. "These blankets belong to these children! Stand aside!"

The coachman cowered below the man-mountain, and stood aside. I collected an extra one for the vicar.

The short trip to the Blything Workhouse was over far too quickly, and our precious time with our mother soon ended, possibly forever, without anything of consequence being said. 'Goodbye', and that was it. So sad. She was taken in by the porter, sporting a club in his belt, and we sat outside in the yard for what seemed a long time, before the vicar held his hand up to the porter and Mum, and we pulled away.

I don't really remember much about my feelings at the time, perhaps for the best. I don't want to remember them, I'm sure they would depress me, so I always remember my mum as Mum, not as goodbye, and the sight of her walking into the workhouse is totally blank. The mind is so clever.

It was really cold up on that open trap, and the vicar stated that we would be on the road for most of the day, so I cuddled tightly with James. Nothing was said for about and hour.

I broke the silence. "Sir, will we be all right?"

He looked sideways at me before nodding. "Of course you will be. The vicar and his wife are kind people, very

charitable, and very well liked in their parish. You'll be fine."
He was quiet for a while as we passed a group of young men.
I noticed that he put his hand down beside the bench,
towards his club. "You can't be too careful out here. Anyway,
Mrs Ashcroft already looks after three children, saved from
their workhouse and children's homes, and I managed to talk
her into taking you two. She could see how beneficial it
would be for all of them to have you there, as you can read
and write so well, and your numbers are exceptional for a
young girl. Peter talked about you all the time. Then, when
you're not teaching the children, you can help Mrs Ashcroft
in the house."

I was a bit surprised at how he spoke of the children,
whilst not including me in the group. "Does she know how
old I am?"

"Of course. You're a young adult. Thirteen. You know, if
you'd gone into the workhouse, you wouldn't be with James,
you'd be working, with the other adults." He sniffed, a
dewdrop forming on the end of his nose. "Warming up a bit.
The sun is a blessing from the Lord, as is life itself."

My heckles suddenly rose. "Sir, why is everything credited
to the Lord? It doesn't make sense. If the Lord can control
things, then why did he take my dad, and Cordelia's dad, and
my two little brothers? Why?" After all these weeks I was
suddenly feeling angry. "Why should I like the Lord when he
doesn't like me? He's left me James, and James me, and
everything else has been taken, and *you* say by the Lord. He's
an evil being if that's how he works." What was I thinking
of? The vicar could have thrown us off his trap and gone
home, leaving a couple of disbelievers stranded at the mercy
of the vagabonds, and God only knows what else. But, he
laughed!

"A chip off the old block!"

He just grinned, as I wondered what he meant, and James
wriggled to wake his bum, which was going numb on the
wooden bench. I always knew of the vicar as being a big man,

but had never before noticed quite how big. Like my dad, he was about five ten, maybe eleven, several inches taller than the average man, and well balanced. He was a very confident individual, and built so similarly to my dad.

"We'll stop for a leg-stretch when we get to Wrentham. Anyway, a chip off the old block, that's you. Strong-headed, intelligent, very handsome or pretty, and issues with the Lord, and you can swing a good right hook. You got her ladyship a good one on the cheek! A miniature Peter Fuller, and that's not an insult. Like your dad, I believe you'll only hit the ones who need it. In all the years I've known your dad, and it's been many, I've never known him to bully anybody, never. Always in charge, but never a bully. You know, I'm going to tell you some things about your dad which you need to know if you're to live in Yarmouth, and I hope James doesn't understand what I'm about to say. Your dad is well known in Yarmouth. Now, when you talk to people about where you're from, be careful about saying who your father was, because some will love him, others will hate him. You might want to call yourselves Ashcroft. Anyway, I grew up with Peter, we were best friends, and both big, strapping lads who would take on anybody, and we did. Eventually we were lured into the Yarmouth fist fights with the gypsies, and made some good money, by always winning."

He stopped for some thoughtful reminiscing, so I quietly told him, "He used to proudly tell me some about the fist fights, and when I suggested that he must have been the best, he always said 'no, second best'. Was he referring to you?"

The vicar nodded. "Yes, but *I'm* not proud of it. In the end we got into some big trouble. We had to stop fighting, and being quite well educated, we both found our callings, me fighting the good fight, and your dad fighting the poachers. Strange where life takes you." He spent a few moments smiling at his own thoughts, while he slowly passed a group of children on their way to school. "I don't know if you know my name, apart from Vicar, but it's Joshua Reed, and, at the time, my uncle was The Sheriff of Suffolk. Anyway, I think he was embarrassed about having a fist-fighter in the family, especially since the gypsies from Norfolk started coming down after our scalps, wanting even bigger return matches, so, in his capacity of the law-keeper of Suffolk, he banned me and Peter from going into Norfolk, for ten years. The ten years were up three years ago, so I can visit our old friend Ashcroft, but Peter never went back. But you *must* be careful if you ever mention his name, or mine, up in Norfolk. The gypsies have long memories."

I felt a warm feeling of pride in my dad's reputation. Most people never ever get noticed, let alone remembered, and it seemed strange to think it, but I really hoped that the Norfolk gypsies would remember him, even if it is for their own reasons of revenge. 'That's my dad!'

We stopped in Wrentham for our leg-stretch, and while the pony was watered and fed the vicar visited one of his acquaintances. We all enjoyed a mug of hot soup. That was when I stopped thinking of my dad, and remembered that my mum and best friend were imprisoned in the workhouse, and my pride swung full circle, emerging as stress and guilt. They were imprisoned, while I sat here enjoying hot drinks, feeding hay to the pony and keeping pleasant company. Right back to the reality of life, remembering that dad is dead, he is the past, and Mum and Cordelia are alive, and they are the present.

Once the pony was happy, we continued our journey north, and we spoke about the workhouse.

Historically, the Bything Workhouse was a good place for the poor, with families living together, all working to create saleable goods, farmed food and dairy products for the residents, and educating the young. When the children reached thirteen years of age, they would be apprenticed to the Bything Hundred Incorporation, and would begin their adult lives outside of the workhouse. It was an institution which helped people when they found themselves at their lowest, the thriving community of about three hundred and fifty people being given help for being poor, not punishment.

Then, about ten years ago, The Blything Hundred Incorporation was dissolved and replaced by the Blything Poor Law Union. It all changed for the worse. The Poor Law Amendment Act of 1834 made sweeping changes to the social care of the poor, taking away all the local benefits given to the poor by the parishes, which were funded by the local poor rate, and made it unlawful to give such benefit. You go to the workhouse, or nothing. Ten years ago the parish of Blythburgh would have helped my mum through her times of despair by way of local support, keeping her out of the workhouse, but now, it's the workhouse or nothing. But, that wasn't all that changed with the new poor law. The major overhaul of the poor laws, all designed in favour of the ruling classes, took away personal pride from the residents of the workhouse and turned them into prisoners, there to serve sentence for the crime of being destitute. One of the many new requirements was that the conditions in the workhouse would be 'less eligible' than those of an independent labourer of the lowest class.

The families and sexes were segregated, the conditions degraded, the freedom curtailed, the diet slashed, and the porters became armed with truncheons. It was turned from being a benevolent institution to a malevolent hellhole, and that was partly what the law was about, punishing people for being really poor, thereby *discouraging* them from being poor. As if they ever had a choice. It was a case of the most powerful, semi-democratic nation in the World being unable to manage their own people. 'If you can't work with them, destroy them.' Echoes of colonialism.

Suddenly the Vicar, Mr Reed, was smiling away to himself. I was sure that I hadn't said anything funny.

"You know, Eunice, you talk very much like a grown up, very mature. But, big but, you need to be careful who you're talking to with your opinionated ideas. Now, I'll ask you a question and you need to answer as if I'm a good friend or family, then again answer as if I'm *not* a good friend nor family. Right, why has your mum gone into the workhouse?"

Well, I had to wonder what he meant, but thought it through, and first gave him my nonfriend-answer. "She has been put into the workhouse because my dad died of the influenza." I took his smile as a pass, then I had to think about telling him my friend-answer. "She was put into the workhouse because my dad had died and we needed work in the house, but could not work in the house because Lord Maybush is a dirty old pervert, so Lady Maybush wouldn't allow me to work in the house. That's the real reason."

I realised what the vicar was teaching me, in that being grown-up is not the same as being adult. It's not just about talking *like* a grown-up, but mostly about saying what an adult would say, the right thing. Adults have had time to learn, and I realised that saying such things about Lord Maybush wouldn't get me into the workhouse, it would be straight into prison. It would almost be juvenile to spout off to a stranger about such things.

"Learn to curb your opinions until they are well thought through. Say what's best for you and James, and forget the rights and wrongs. Survival is more likely as an adult, not just as a grown-up."

Good advice from the former fist-fighter and man of God.

"Anyway, because I'm a family friend, and I owe it to Peter, I think I should tell you why I think your mum is in the workhouse. It's because of you and James." He stopped for effect, and it worked! "She *volunteered* for the workhouse, so that you and James could live a better life. You see, Eunice, another thing that was established by the recent poor laws was that it was voluntary to go into the workhouse, and if you refused you would receive no further help. Now, if you do volunteer for the workhouse, you are then deemed to be incapable of looking after yourself outside of the workhouse, and essentially you were there for life. It's become a no-win situation. Unless something came along to prove that you would be looked after outside of the workhouse, they won't let you out. A life sentence. Now, your mum agreed to go in, after that initial rejection from her, but she knew what was happening, and made her decision. She did it for you. Now, go and make her proud of her decision, by having a good life, both of you. Live for her, be happy, but never feel guilty, as she knew exactly what she was doing."

I had a lot of growing up to do, quickly, but was learning to be an adult. In a nutshell, my Dad's life-long friend was giving us a massive leg up out of the hole that we had been thrown into, and I felt that I had to take advantage of it, for me *and* James, and you never know, 'perhaps I can get my mummy out of the workhouse, even Cordelia'. I felt more hopeful than I'd felt since Dad's death, and I even felt warm, cuddled with James, and safe, sitting beside an ex-fist fight champ. Life will be good again.

Peter Fuller's Daughter

CHAPTER 7
IN HIDING

Mr Reed made another stop when we reached Lowestoft. The horses were watered and fed some hay, then he visited yet another of his church colleagues who gave us soup and bread. We were getting close to our destination, but we got back onto the dusty road as soon as ready, as it was threatening to get dark.

"Don't want you two on the roads at night. Come on."

The roads were dry, so we were making good time, and would soon be on the outskirts of Yarmouth where the Ashcrofts lived, our new home.

"Do you think, Mr Reed, that I'll be able to get Mum out of the workhouse? If I dream it, do you think I could *ever* do it?"

He suddenly looked sternly at me, straight in the eye. "Now, young lady, I'll only say this once! I'm a life-long friend of your dad's, so my name is *Joshua*!" He grinned, and his tone changed. "Of course you will. You're Peter's daughter, so you'll never give up. Just try to be a little less unpopular than he made himself."

"How, Joshua?" I smiled back at him. "What do I do to be less unpopular?"

"Well, don't do what he did. If you have to go into hiding, as he had to, remember to drop the disguise when amongst friends and family. He took his act too far at times, and everyone believed in his act. You know what, Lord Maybush gave him the job because the previous manager was weak, and they all walked over him, but Peter was hard, feared nobody, and that was what he was in everybody's eyes, including Lord Maybush's. A controlling bully, but it all was just a front. But, Maybush also had another reason to stick with your dad; he won handsomely on a bet on something which your dad did many years ago. A very big win. So, Peter took a job with Lord Maybush, and took his job seriously, sometimes too seriously, and I think he became known as his disguise, a bully, and, from the moment he raised his disguise, *nobody* ever really knew Peter Fuller. You know as well as anybody that he'd do anything for his loved ones, but others never saw it. And the layman preaching? It was for his friend…. It was for me. When I was ordained, the workhouse became one of my flock, and I had instruction from Ipswich to toe the party line, making sure everybody knows what the new laws required of a workhouse: discouragement. Make sure nobody ever wanted to go into the workhouse, and Peter volunteered to do it for me, because he knew that I couldn't. He preached down to the residents, blaming them all for what has happened to them, all self-inflicted. You reap what you sow, and all that shit. But he *never* believed it. It was all part of his disguise."

"But, why did he make *us* believe it? I enjoyed the bible lessons, they taught us all to read and write, and silly examples like the money lenders, to help us with our numbers, but he always made us think he believed it all. I *believed* he was a bible-bashing bigot at the workhouse. Why fool me?"

He shook his head several times. I thought he was not going to answer my question, but, "I told you about my uncle, John Reed, The Sheriff of Suffolk, who banned us from entering Norfolk for ten years. Well, the trouble all started when Peter beat one of the Norfolk Taylor gypsies. Your dad was hurt badly, but his opponent was hurt much worse, and died several weeks later from his injuries, and so his family came south in search of Peter. That's when we took our own roads to that new life, me hiding in the church, him in the control of others as the Maybush manager. He spent the rest of his life afraid, not of fighting, but of his family getting hurt in the battle. He learned to live his disguise in fear of his family's safety. It was *always* for his family." He was quiet, in thought, for a few minutes, then, "And for me. Your dad was an absolute hero, a martyr, who lived the rest of his life for others, and perhaps forgetting his real self. When they came looking for both of us, it was really him they were after, but I never let him suffer it alone. He was the closest thing I've ever had to a brother, and that was for life, so, when Ipswich ordered me to teach the workhouse residents why they were there, I couldn't do it. It's all a lie, in most cases, pure brainwashing of the peasants. So, like a real brother, Peter volunteered as a layman preacher, and did it for me. It saved me from lying to those poor souls…. He never believed any of it, it was all for me, and for you. Just part of his disguise, and he never let it slip. Peter Fuller died thirteen years ago, and was reborn as your dad. Perhaps that's what reincarnation really is. Anyway, his plan worked, perfectly." His head nodded a few times. "Perhaps he *did* do it right, living the disguise to protect his family. But, what a cost."

I saw Mr Reed's face, and it looked away. I was sure that he had a tear on his cheek, but it could have been the cold breeze.

"Sorry, we went off the subject a bit. Your mum? Never give up trying, your dad never would, but be careful with your dreams." He shook his head a few times, before saying very carefully, "In my job I see a lot of hope in people, and lot of despair, so, never give up on your dreams, but *never* lose sight of reality. I've seen many a dead dreamer."

A bit like Cordelia's uncle, in Bolivia. I promised myself to dwell on that one. "Thank you, Joshua."

The trap eventually pulled up outside the vicarage as the sun was dropping. It was a nice house, rendered and whitewashed with thatched roof, and with its own stoned drive-way and a cut lawn in the middle. It was much bigger than our manager's house, advertising the Church of England's rich power. Joshua alighted and pulled the door bell.

Almost immediately the front door swung open and there stood a lanky vicar. He was drawn, starting to go grey, and looked like he could do with a good meal, but his smile was welcoming.

"Joshua! Glad you made it before dark. There's been a lot of night-time robberies along the Lowestoft Road, so I hope you're staying until morning."

They shook hands as a middle-aged lady appeared behind him. She looked a lot better fed than Mr Ashcroft, with a sterner look, but smiled as she took James by the hand. Our new 'mum' led us into the house, and, as the sun was just dropping, the oil lamps were lit in the hall. But it was still dingy and cold. It reminded me of the church, almost as cold as it was outside, and I wondered if it was a Godly thing to be cold in both the churches and in the vicarages. I reminded myself to ask Joshua about it, if I ever got the chance.

Anyway, we had arrived at our new home, and I felt a little excited, although wary, but Mrs Ashcroft welcomed us kindly, and led us through into the kitchen. It was spacious, with a scrubbed pine dining table in front of the window, and a large inglenook fireplace opposite. The fire was burning well, with a supply of logs piled to the left and a swinging pot-gantry to the right, with several large pots beneath it. Hanging above the hot embers was a smaller pot with what smelled like sprouts simmering. Opposite the entrance was a large pantry, but, apart from a dresser beside the pantry, there was little else in the room. Oh, apart from, of course, three children sitting at the table, eating a bread and cheese supper. Two boys and a girl, all about the same age as James, and they took him in like they already knew him, giving him some of their bread and cheese, before taking him up to bed with them. Mrs Ashcroft followed and I followed her, then she showed me my little room, in the attic, at one end of the gable. It had a small window, but I was unable to see what was outside.

"Mr Ashcroft has been quite excited about you coming.

He knew your dad quite well, many years ago, and recently they've used the new postal system to write to each other. He feels that he already knows you, as your dad spoke a lot about you in his letters. So, he wants you to supper with him and Mr Reed, like an adult."

I suddenly felt like more than just a child, sitting around the fire with the men and talking the good talk. I was intrigued to know what vicars talked about amongst themselves.

Along with the men, we sat at the table in the kitchen and ate a modest meal of potatoes, salted pork and sprouts, before moving into the sitting room, around the small fireplace. The seats were wing-backs, very comfortable, warm and seemed expensive, each with a pedestal side-table, and a matching pair of mahogany lowboys flanked the fireplace. Mrs Ashcroft left us to it.

"Well, Eunice, it's lovely to meet you at last, after a couple of years of just hearing about you from your dad." Mr Ashcroft, skinny and grey, nodded and smiled. "It's very difficult to do verbal justice to one so pretty. You're even prettier than he described you."

Joshua looked me in the face and raised his eyebrows. I think he was saying 'be careful'.

"Anyway, I like to comfort my malaria with a whisky or two in the evening. You two must join me." He went to one of the lowboys, and returned with a decanter of whisky and three glasses. "Cheers!"

I felt obliged to take a small one, and the first was a shot-drink, raised to the queen then straight down, and the glasses banged on the side-tables. Poor James must have thought the poachers were out when he heard the shots. We all grimaced at the harshness of the local whisky, but still took a refill.

"Anyway, Eunice, I'm a Lanky soldier with malaria, which is why I'm so skinny. Hope that doesn't put you off me."

I had no idea what that meant, until I received the raised eyebrows from Joshua, silently saying 'be careful', again.

Mr Ashcroft explained to me that he had joined the King's army after becoming ordained, as an army chaplain, and had forevermore regretted it, since he was immediately posted to Sri Lanka to do his duty in the Kandyan Wars. The war was gruelling, fought mainly on the thickly forested hillsides, and could well be described as gorilla warfare. He said that half the time they were fighting an invisible enemy who would appear, do their damage, and immediately disappear. The conditions were so bad that, when the regiment returned from Sri Lanka to Aston, they were all so skinny, undernourished, diseased and battle damaged, that they were nicknamed 'Lanky' soldiers, and the nickname for skinny men has stuck, ever since.

"So, I don't mind you calling me Lanky." He went on to explain that it was all the army left him with when they kicked him out on ill health. "It's a constant reminder of how good life can be here, compared to that of a Blighty in India. I was approached by the East India Company and offered a job in their army, but I don't think I could handle another stint in India. Nor China."

We talked about the local fish industry, which was on its knees due to overfishing and foreign intrusions, and the recent storm which took many fishermen's lives, and about him teaching me to scythe the front lawn, but nothing about the bible or God or the church. It was quite refreshing, especially after a few more whiskies, and I felt a little heady by the end of the evening. I also felt a tiny bit uneasy. I constantly felt Lanky's eyes burning into me. I hoped that this wasn't to be a 'Lord Maybush'. Again, Joshua raised his eyebrows at me.

We all arose the next morning at the crack of dawn, and Mrs Ashcroft took me under her wing to show me the ropes in the kitchen and around the house. James was surprisingly excited about his new family, especially the girl, who was quieter than the boys and looked like she was looking for a soul to be in her corner with her, and she saw James as her ally. Perhaps we can be happy again, like the red squirrel, and make our nests right here, in Yarmouth. Then, as we entered the sitting room, Lanky was putting the whisky away, into the lowboy, right where I had already put it last night before going to bed. He still smelled of the spirit, even above his body odours. I promised to store that one for future reference.

Then, Joshua came downstairs, ready to leave. He made sure that he took me aside for a private goodbye. "I hope I haven't put you into a bad spot. I've seen his looks towards you."

"So have I. I've felt them, but I'll be all right, promise." I almost clammed up, but, "If I'd gone into the big house, Lord Maybush would've been the same." I perhaps shouldn't have said that.

"It's all right, I know what his Lordship's like. If you have any problems with Lanky, write to me." He gave me a sheet of paper with his address on, and two penny-black stamps. "Stay out of his way, if you can. And never forget, we're family."

Peter Fuller's Daughter

CHAPTER 8
TO DREAM OR NOT TO DREAM

The next four months drifted by, with me and James settling in with our new family. He was in his element, falling madly in love with his new brothers and sister, and striking up a seriously close relationship with Brenda, the girl of the group. They were almost inseparable.

My duties were those of an adult, which I can't complain about as I was thirteen, and my tutoring of the children was something that I'll never forget, absolutely loving that feeling of giving them something to take with them through their entire lives. The only problem, at times, was breaking up the monotony of brainwashing with some form of interest. My dad kept us interested in reading by using stories, so, I turned to the bible stories which I knew so well from my own education, and the children hung on in there. Within about three months they were showing outstanding improvements, reading short passages from various books, and understanding what they were reading. The one dragging behind was Brenda. Poor James, he was suffering for his soulmate, giving her encouragement, help, and, I think, love.

I couldn't help but to see me and Cordelia sitting there. Brenda was very plain, not academically gifted, just like Cordelia, and James loved her like a sister, as I loved Cordelia. I burst into tears.

The older of the boys grabbed my hand and led me upstairs to my room. He left me sobbing.

"Eunice, what's this?" Mrs Ashcroft stomped into my room. "You've left the children alone! What're you doing?"

As I looked round at her she saw the tears, and sat down beside me on the bed. She seemed to have to force herself, but she put her arm around my shoulders and pulled me in.

In her broad Norfolk accent, "What's the matter? Has Mr Ashcroft been up to mischief, again?"

"No! No, definitely not, he's been a perfect gentleman. Please don't blame him." I had to think about what the matter was, but it was all a mist. "Not sure. I just miss my mum and Cordelia so much." I was still snivelling between words. "Something struck me. Yes, Brenda and James, they suddenly reminded me of me and Cordelia, and I…." I didn't know what to say, but then it came to me. "I should be with Mum and Cordelia, in the workhouse."

"Don't be stupid!" Her stern face almost scowled. "That's the most stupidest thing I've ever heard in my life! Now, get down there with the children and don't *ever* talk like that again!" She pushed me away, tutted, then suddenly stopped. "Stupid! Think before you speak, or the good Lord'll hear you. He's always listening, and don't talk to anybody else about that sort of thing, *ever*. They'll think you're an imbecile and lock you away, and it won't be in with your mum, believe you me. They've got a place down the road where that sort of talk leads you. Honestly!" She stood up, then just looked down at me for a while, before leaving the room.

That was what I needed, a kick up the arse, reminding me that James and I were so lucky to be where we were, and, although I knew that I should never give up on being with Mum and Cordelia, I should never give up on James: I had made a promise to look after him. But the wise words of my friend Joshua would never go away. 'Never give up on your dreams, but never lose sight of reality.' So, I needed to keep a balanced ambition, since I wasn't ready to die. 'Thank you Joshua.'

"Yes, if I can do well in life, I can get them out." I convinced myself that that was the answer to mine and my family's happiness, get them out, not join them. It all seemed so simple in the dream.

In the reality part of the ambition, I set myself the goal of tutoring the four children to a level where they could themselves do well in life, and I found it especially rewarding. I began to feel that I had a calling, one which would pay towards my family's reunion.

Mrs Ashcroft gradually became closer in her manner towards me, and I came to look forward to our work in the kitchen, especially on wash-days. Once we had swung the boiling pot over the fire, we would sit at the table and talk. It became our time together, and we made productive use of the intimacy. She had a very soft voice, which seldom seemed to match her sternness, and I felt that there was a contradiction in that she was broad Norfolk, but well spoken. If you heard her talking in the middle of Yarmouth, you may think that she is not from around here, but with the same accent. Strange.

Anyway, it turned out that she was barren, and the more we spoke, the more she revealed about her deepest self. It seemed to me that she hadn't talked deeply to anybody for a long time, maybe never, and I was there to furnish that release. She told me about her childhood, in the Norwich Workhouse, and about how many bad memories she had of her treatment there, but she was not prepared to go into detail. She just told me, in no uncertain terms, that I should never wish to go there; pure stupidity.

As she turned thirteen she was taken on in one of the silk factories in Norwich, and found lodgings on the edge of The Tomb, and while there, a young man was visiting the works in the cathedral, work which involved the creation of Norwich Cathedral's Lady Chapel, and it was Mr Ashcroft.

"He was a stunning young man, tall, dark and full, and when we were introduced, we fell instantly in love. I think he was a childhood friend of your dad and Mr Reed, but he went straight into the church from school, unlike your dad and Joshua. He never liked fist-fighting, so stayed out of their way for a while. We married. Anyway, just as I thought we were to move down into Suffolk, in a parish of our own, he joined the army, the Rutlandshires, and was posted to Ceylon." She remained quiet, in deep thought, for some time, then, "I think he went to get away from me, but he always denied that. Then, when he came home he was demobbed from the army on ill-health, and continued his role in civilian life, here. He was very unhealthy. He almost died from the malaria, and you can see what he's like now. He lives on quinine, laudanum and whisky, and now he blames me for not giving him a family. You know, we just exist for the sake of his reputation within the church, and even that is rapidly depleting with every case of whisky. I wonder how much longer…." But she said no more about her unhappy marriage. "Please don't talk to anybody else about these things."

However, she did say how proud she was of me for rejecting Mr Ashcroft's hands from my breasts, while he was teaching me to use the scythe on the lawn. I never knew she was watching, but once I did know, I felt a bit safer in his presence.

One morning, as the four children brought logs in from the back, I boiled the drinking water. I kept a close eye on the four of them, as they had developed a mischievous attitude to something in the back garden. To get to the garden from the kitchen one had to leave the room, turn left away from the front door, to the back door. As I was watching them in the garden Mrs Ashcroft made me jump from behind, from the front door. She looked almost as mischievous as the children, and beckoned me to the table.

"There's not much harm they can do out there, so sit with me, please." She grinned.

She had just returned from her charity work, with the District Visiting Society, and looked so pleased with herself, but said nothing, so I asked, "How are the Grahams?" They were a family who had just lost their father and two oldest sons to a recent storm. Not uncommon in a fishing community.

"They're holding up, you know how it is, and we've just

raised enough to give the men a decent burial. Now the children in the next room are suffering with small-pox. I was pleased to get out of there." She hesitated, and forced a smile. "I can't afford to take all the children, but look at this." She unfolded a poster which she'd been asked to put on the church noticeboard, and laid it out in front of me.

The circus was coming to town!

"I can't take *all* the children, so I can't take *any*, but we can take them to…. Look at the bottom part!"

Nelson the Clown! On Friday the second of May, he was to do his usual thing in promoting the circus and a testimonial show, by sailing up the river in a tub, pulled by a team of geese.

"We can get there early and watch from the bridge. Mrs Graham said it's loved by all the children."

"But," I hesitated, "don't you have to pay to go over the bridge? For all of us it would be threepence."

"No, Mrs Graham said that it costs a halfpenny each to go over the bridge, but the tollgate is the *other* side, so, we can go *onto* the bridge without going past the toll. She says we won't have to pay. There's talk about them stopping the charges for foot-crossers, anyway." With a big look of expectancy, she asked me, "Well, should we do it?"

She was asking *me*, almost begging for permission. It gave me a very, very strange feeling, one which spanned several emotions, such as surprise, confusion, pride, and satisfaction, and my head spun for few seconds as I felt a doomful abode in my heart. I didn't want to do it, but, "Yes, if you think we should. The children'll love it, I think."

She took that as my blessing, but it left me with a sadness which seemed so unexplainable, and I briefly wished that Joshua was around for me to talk to.

Peter Fuller's Daughter

CHAPTER 9
TOGETHERNESS

When Mrs Ashcroft told the children about our day out with Nelson the Clown, they were duly excited, and became a bit of a handful at times, playing around while I was trying to teach, talking when I was trying to explain, and just being disrespectful to their teacher, me. Eventually I had to say it.

"Shut....up!" I slapped the ruler across the palm of my hand, and they froze. "You're not too big to get this across your asses, so, shut....up!" It worked, for a while, just long enough to get through the story of David and Goliath, before they lost interest and were again fidgety. "I think we'll call it a day, and resume tomorrow, but, before we go, some sums. To go over the bridge, it costs a halfpenny each. There'll be six of us, and if I only have a shilling in my purse, how much change will I get? Six crossing, how much change from a shilling? Write down the answer." I looked into their faces, and the boys had all worked it out quickly, but Brenda was looking confused. I shook my head at James, to stop him telling her, then asked, "Brenda, how many pennies in a shilling?" She quietly answered twelve. "And how much for six of us across the bridge?" She counted it out on her fingers, and quietly answered three. "So, three pennies from twelve leaves…?"

I could see her brain working, then her face lit up. "Nine! Ninepence change." It made her day, especially when James chirped up with his answer, which was wrong. "I beat James to the answer!"

I do believe that he deliberately let her win, and why not? He wanted to do anything to make Brenda happy, and it showed as he constantly boosted her confidence, supported her and stood her corner. He suddenly stated, "I don't want to go to see Nelson. It'll be boring."

I couldn't believe what I was hearing, so I just looked hard into his face.

"Me and Brenda can wait here, at home, while you all go."

I was astonished, but felt that there had to be a reason, so I asked him if he was telling the truth, the whole truth, and after a bit of fidgeting, he told me, "Brenda can't go. She's scared, so can't go, so, I can't go."

I dismissed the group, and they all went out into the garden to get some spring sun. But I kept Brenda behind for a chat. She sheepishly cuddled up to me, and told me why she was so scared. Her family were fishermen, and all but her and her mum were lost during the big storm of eighteen forty-four, just last year, then her mum died. So, she was afraid of standing over water, she could drown, as her dad and brothers and uncle had. But, she had a *new* brother.

"If it means a lot to James, I can come on the bridge, but not look down. I'll try."

We would have to take it as it comes, on the day, and stand by her. If we had to watch from the quay, we could still see Nelson sail by, no big deal, but it *was* a big deal to Brenda, so we had to stick by her. We all had two weeks to dwell on it, and besides, they may not even let us on the bridge without paying our threepence, and Mrs Ashcroft had already indicated that the threepence would need to go towards Lanky's whisky. For the sake of Lanky and Brenda, perhaps that would be the moral thing to do, stay on dry land, on the quay.

Well, we had two weeks to wait for the big occasion, in the meantime, spring was in the air, arousing the grass into growth and sparking spring fever in Mr Ashcroft. He always insisted on me calling him Lanky when we were alone, so I did, since it was easy compared to what he was really after, and when he called me to help him with the scything of the lawn, I prepared myself, not for what he was after, but for the fight which would prevail when his hands wandered. I was determined to smack him across the head, or in the groin, if he tried anything.

I really wanted to wait for him to make his move, so that I could knee him hard in the knackers and feel good, a lot of Dad in me, but I realised that it wasn't that simple. He would throw me out, and I may never see James again. So, another plan.

He had waited for Mrs Ashcroft to go off on her charity meet before calling me, as he must have known she was watching the previous time, so I used the children as my shield.

"I can't leave the children alone for all that time. They can come out and watch me swing the scythe."

It was my second lesson in lawn-cutting, so the first job was to whet the scythe, ensuring a razor-sharp edge, and it was something that Dad had already taught me, so, I was quite good with the stone, and was soon ready for the cut, poised. I stopped him from putting his arms around me from the back, as I insisted that I had already done that lesson and could swing the scythe quite competently. He looked around at the watching children, then stood aside, with a slight grumble below his breath. Then I started the job. The grass was growing strongly, and was tender, so the scythe sliced through the blades with ease, and I felt so proud of my swing, which was a combination of body and arm movement. I felt so satisfied. It was, as Lanky had said before, very good therapy.

"Stop there!" He stepped to me, and put his hand out for the scythe. "That's a good patch. I'll show you how it should be done, and the children can judge." He was a lot taller than me, so had a much broader swing, one which he had practiced for many years, and his patch was just about perfect. He stood up straight, looked to the children with a cocky air, "Right you lot. Look at the two patches, and tell me which is the best. Which one of us is the lawn-king?"

They all looked at Lanky, then at me, then put their heads together to discuss the judgment. The oldest boy, Stephen, stood forward.

"Eunice is the king! Her's is best, by miles."

They all giggled, but Lanky did not. He threw the scythe onto the ground, stepped to the boy and hit him so hard across the side of the head that he was knocked to the ground. The other three ran to the house.

"What the hell you doing?" I screeched, and stepped towards him, fists clenched and knee waiting. "Leave him alone, or else!"

He turned on me and raised his hand, but then noticed the children who watched from the road, and he seemed to remember that he was a vicar, a man of God. He stormed into the house, then my other children ran back out.

It was all over in a minute or so, but it taught me a very big lesson about Mr Ashcroft and his addictions, and I realised that he was not going to get any better, then, when the children on the road began talking about him loud enough for me to hear, I learned a little bit about the reputation that he was developing. While helping Stephen up, I made my mind up that we would find somewhere else to live before Lanky was thrown out of the church and his house, which would probably put us into the workhouse. Yes, a proactive approach was needed. Be in control.

I spoke privately with the children, and they agreed not to say anything to Mrs Ashcroft about Stephen being hit by Lanky, and they seemed to understand how he should never have done it without any reason. He only did it because I beat him, despite my patch not being anywhere near as perfect as his, and perhaps he knew that it wasn't a vote in my favour, but a vote against him. The children never said anything, but I sensed that this wasn't the first time that he had hit them.

"One day we can find a home of our own, all of us, with Mum and Cordelia." James agreed wholeheartedly that we should at least try. They were all frightened of what their foster father could do when drunk. He was drunk most of the time, and if not, stoned on the laudanum. A dangerous man amongst vulnerable people.

"What about Mrs Ashcroft?" Stephen had a spot for her in his heart. "She's not much fun, but she's nice and kind."

So, my dream was slowly developing, growing bigger by the day, but it was going to be a mammoth task to turn it into reality.

I decided to write to Joshua, as a starter. I needed to tell somebody about Lanky and our plan, and he was the only man I trusted at the time. I had two black stamps in my purse, which Joshua had given me in case of emergency, and I believed that this constituted an emergency.

The very next day, as the sun rose above the distant North Sea, Mrs Ashcroft exploded. She saw Stephen's face which had swelled up overnight.

"What the hell has happened, Stephen?" She pulled him in for a soothing cuddle, before giving the injury a proper check over.

"I fell over when we were bringing logs in."

She never believed him, but said nothing else, quietly putting a cold, damp cloth over the bruise.

I realised we were a real team, us children, but I felt a little guilty that we hadn't told Mrs Ashcroft the truth, as she was our friend and family. But she was married to a vicar, an alcoholic whose brain was becoming fuzzled and his manner perverse, and she was compelled to stick by him. That was expected of the class of person that she had married into, the middle class, neither gentry nor pauper, and their only brag is that they have superior moral standards; poppy cock! You have to look a bit deeper than their façade to see the real morals, and then you'll see that they're no different to the soak-heads in the slums. Alcohol and opium have no barriers, and favour no flag.

Peter Fuller's Daughter

CHAPTER 10
THE WHISKY JAR, OR, SADISTIC SATISFACTION

Not much happened over the next two weeks, as we waited for Nelson's gargantuan show of bravery and stupidity, but, all joking aside, that's what clowns are bred for, acting stupidly. It seemed to appeal to all ages of mankind.

The main reportable event of the two weeks came about due to Lanky's whisky habit. Mrs Ashcroft suggested that we all walk with her to the distiller, to collect Lanky's whisky ration for the week, joking that it would save her having to carry it all herself. She would carry three stone jars, I would carry three, and the four children, one each, all in strong hessian bags. That was the first that we knew how much he drank each week, ten jars, probably almost ten pints in total. Of course, we had to take ten stone jars back, the empties, so we got in some practice on the outbound trip. We all raised our eyebrows at each other when about halfway, knowing that the full ones would be a lot heavier for the return trip, and the straps on the bags were already cutting into the children's hands.

"See what I have to put up with each week, on my own." Mrs Ashcroft almost swore under her breath. "Old Swilley used to deliver, until Mr Ashcroft was always drunk when he turned up, and kept insulting the old man. He won't deliver now, even for a couple of pennies."

"Why don't we make a barrow? It can be part of the children's schooling, the sort of thing we had to learn on the Estate farm." I nodded and smiled as she thought about it, then she smiled back, so, "Right, our next school project, design and build a whisky barrow."

We had to pass Mr Ashcroft's church, then several nice, medium-sized houses which were all thatched with Norfolk reed, and some open space which was being farmed, before hitting the edge of the town-proper. The dirt road was dry that day, but it was always very muddy when wet, even with the clinkers that the council spread, and there was a surprising amount of traffic in both directions. Some of the carts where well laden, and the horses sweated as they pulled past us, the sweet smell reminding me of home. However much I get used this town-life, it will never be the same as home, in the quiet of the countryside, with the space, the privacy, and the tender smells of nature. The town of Yarmouth just smelled of fish and sewerage!

I realised how fortunate the folk from the countryside were, with a bit of space around them, no money nor luxuries, but fresh air and freedom. Cordelia's little house was tiny compared to ours, but it had its own space in this world, with room to bury their waste, and to walk quietly, but here, the tiny houses are crammed together with a ditch running past the front for the poo and piss to be chucked into, and they still didn't have any money nor luxuries. It seemed that the only aim in life for many of these people was to feed themselves and their families, and to buy the beer which they drank because the water was so poisonous. A life on the waves, and probably a death on the waves, was all they could be proud of, just to catch enough herring or mackerel to survive; nothing else in life, apart from the pox-scars. But, of course, that was only three quarters of the population, and the others? They had something, at least, and I was just beginning to realise what that something was. It was a standing in life, a good name, pride and prejudice, a face to keep up, a place to hang onto in society, like poor Mrs Ashcroft who suffered because of the good name and reputation of her drunken husband. It was all about maintaining your place in the tribe's pecking order. She should come with us when we leave, and be part of our tribe and that was something to touch upon one of these days, around the kitchen table.

Anyway, we eventually arrived at the distillers. The front entrance was the only way in from the front of the brick building, and had we not have already known that it was a distillery, we never would have known. We entered into a small room where a lady sat behind a desk, and after a nod from her, stood our empty jars down in the corner. It had a strong feeling of high security, with a burley man standing by the door to the warehouse.

"Good morning Mrs Ashcroft. Brought the whole tribe with you, I see. And two new ones!"

Mrs Ashcroft introduce me and James, then the whisky-seller shouted through the door, before sitting back at her desk. "Your boy's got a fair old bruise coming." She looked at Stephen, who looked at the ground. "How'd you get that?"

Stephen felt obliged to answer the questions of an adult. "I bashed it in the garden, when we were getting the logs in."

Then a boy came in from the warehouse, with a sack barrow loaded with stone jars. He carefully unloaded them from the barrow, ready for us to carry home. But before he went back to the warehouse, I realised that it was one of the boys who had watched Lanky hit Stephen.

He was a bit older than our boys, and probably a bit wiser. "Won't be long, mush. Soon be able to hit him back." Then he went.

Suddenly I could feel Mrs Ashcroft screwing my head, and I knew exactly what she was thinking.

"Eunice, take the children outside with their jars. I need to talk to Maisie."

We put our jars into our bags, and got out, but never had to wait for long. She looked very calm.

"Let's walk behind the children. They know the way." We hung back, as I waited for the scolding. "So, he hit him. Why didn't you tell me?"

She never seemed to be mad at me, so I felt it safe to tell the truth.

"Although he doesn't deserve respect, I thought that the

boys' advice was good, just to keep quiet and not cause any more trouble. Let him get away with it, this time."

"I know you did it for the right reasons, but you've got to remember what he is, a drunken, dangerous, knackered, old soak. He can't keep getting away with it, and perhaps the boys didn't tell you that this has happened several times before, always for no reason, so this isn't the first time and won't be the last. There's been quite a few, and these boys don't do anything to deserve a hiding or thump, but he still gives it to them. He's dangerous." She sniffed. "I don't know what to do."

Children are there to supply the world with new grown-ups, little else, so they aren't that important in the bigger picture. They're a product which is still in the process of manufacture, so a bit of rough is all part of their development into manhood, but I can't ever accept that those men, nor women, should get satisfaction from the beating of a child, even if he does deserve it. Sadistic satisfaction is cruel and dangerous, as is old Lanky.

"You know," I hesitated before continuing, "we have spoke about leaving. You've given us a home and food and some love, and we're so lucky to have this second chance, but...."

"I know. I know what you're going to say, I've lived it for years, and I know. He'll only get worse. And Maisie said that he is getting himself a poor name in the community, turning into a vicar who carries no respect, and she thinks that they'll replace him one of these days. Then what?"

We caught the children up, as they had to stop for a rest. The jars were much heavier with whisky inside!

CHAPTER 11
THE BRIDGE

The atmosphere changed from that point. Although we had never seriously discussed our leaving with Mrs Ashctoft, the little hint which I had left her during the whisky trip definitely sank in. She had this air about her which wafted more towards us children than towards Lanky Ashcroft, and I could feel that she was looking for a new nest. In just a day she had become attached to us, not just as our surrogate keeper, but as an equal. We all needed each other. But, the children had other things on their minds, Nelson the Clown's testimonial river stunt. The annual water frolic.

Mrs Ashcroft had been talking to her friend in the Lines, and had found out that Nelson wasn't doing the stunt for charitable reasons, but as an advertisement for his testimonial show, to be performed that very evening. The stunt was hopefully to attract a large crowd to that night's performance in The Wintergarden, and his loyal service over the years with Cooke's circus gave him the privilege of receiving the night's entire takings. It was his retirement benefit. Cooke's was a renowned circus throughout many parts of the World, Nelson being a well respected performer.

The morning of the great feat soon arrived, and it was dull, overcast, with just a little spray in the air, but our appetite for the trip was never dented. With some buttered bread and boiled eggs in a bag, and safe water in two jars, we set off. It would take a little while to walk to the docks and we wanted to make sure that we could find a good viewpoint, so gave it a couple of hours, and I stopped into the Mayor's office to check for any post for me, as I still hadn't heard back from Joshua, but nothing had come. With the damp, heavy air the streets, houses and businesses smelled rancid and dank, and for some unexplainable reason I was feeling the same, rancid and dank, just for a fleeting moment. I had a niggling feeling of fear for our future, and, not for the first time, I began to wonder if we should have gone into the workhouse with Mum. I looked at Mrs Ashcroft, but said nothing.

However, she did say something. "You need to be very careful with this thing about leaving. Look at these streets, depressing, diseased, violent and these people really struggle to get out of these tiny hovels; it's for life. Is that what you want?"

"No, but I don't want to be kicked out when Mr Ashcroft is relieved of his duties. That would put us in a desperate spot and we *would* end up in these streets, or the workhouse, so I think we should act before it happens, and be in control. Proactive, as my dad used to say."

She shook her head, then huffed. "I should come with you, if you'll have me."

I just answered with a smile of support, and we walked on.

As we approached the river, the boys ran ahead to look out at the fishing boats and wherries which were moored in the basin, towards Breydon Water. They were all bow-facing downriver, as the tide had begun to run in, so it wouldn't be long before Nelson would be sailing up-tide with the flood. We stopped for a few moments while the boys looked out, dreaming of adventure. Brenda had seen many a fishing boat, good and bad, and was no longer a fan, so stayed back with us.

"I think I can come on the bridge." She spoke nervously. "James has promised to hold my hand, and look after me." They often spoke like a tiny couple, married or courting, not sure which, but together. We each held one of her hands as she nervously smiled up at us.

"I think James likes me a lot. He's kind."

As his doting sister, "I couldn't agree more."

Then, Mrs Ashcroft gave her a sideways cuddle and

smiled towards me.

Anyway, the boys had seen enough and were back, so we marched on towards the bridge, past the quay which stunk of mackerel, and joined the migrating crowd. People were beginning to turn up in their throngs, some in large groups of children, presumably from orphanages and schools, and the bridge had started to fill up. I ran ahead to find an adult to ask about paying, and she told me that they weren't taking any money, so long as we don't go across the other side, near the toll-booth. As I headed back to the others, a cart was coming from the Acle side, the horse being very wary not to tread on the small children. The coachman shouted as he reached our side of the river, "Tide's turned. Soon be here!" and waved his hand at the crowd. So we found our spot on the bridge, against the railings, looking downriver towards Breydon Water. We waited.

It wasn't a giant bridge, looked like about five rods long, *(about-eighty five feet),* with a large tower each end. Between the towers were two rod-and-eye chains, seven feet apart, and from those chains the bridge was suspended by steel rods. Each side of the seven-foot bridge, a footpath had been added, each about four feet wide. I'm no engineer, but the added footpaths never looked like they belonged. They looked as though they were after-thoughts, as they were, and the whole set-up appeared to be unbalanced.

It had been the centre of attention for some years, with the owner jealously protecting his investment against the onslaught of the new transport system, the railway, which had finally received permission to come to Yarmouth. The case had been in and out of court and parliament for some years, but progress marches on. George Stephenson's railways had won, to the benefit of the town, so, another bridge was to be built conveniently closer to the rail terminal, to connect it to the town. Yarmouth was segregated from Norwich, and the rest of England, by the Bure and the Yare, and the main means of transport into the rest of the country was either by boat via the River Yare, or by cart across our bridge and onto the Acle Turnpike. The railways would transform the entire distribution system, enabling the mackerel and herring catches to be swiftly delivered to the markets, as well as facilitating the distribution of the coal, steel and stone which would come into the Yarmouth docks. The town desperately needed a kick in the right direction, as recent years, since the end of the Napoleonic Wars, had seen many a hardship. The suspension bridge had offered essential contact routes with the rest of the country, but now seemed to be living out its final years. The railway is progress, and will change the economic geography of the whole of Great Britain and the World, and there was no stopping it now.

But the new bridge was yet to be built, and so the suspension bridge still had its uses, including that of a viewing stage for Nelson's stunt. Hundreds of children and adults made use of it on that day, as they all enthusiastically awaited his approach, along with hundreds more who had lined the quaysides.

We were lucky to find a spot against the railings facing downriver, which was to be where Nelson would first appear as he rode the flood tide from Breydon Water. Mrs Ashcroft held the hands of the two boys, while I held those of James and Brenda. We had to stand firm in order not to lose our spot at the front of the crowd, especially when a man from the quay shouted that he was on his way, but the excitement soon quelled when it was reported that Nelson had missed his turn into the Bure, and had been pushed by the tide up the Yare. Eventually it was reported that he had been pulled back to the mouth of the Bure.

"You know," Mrs Ashcroft whispered in my ear, "the geese aren't really pulling him, there's a rope under the water, tied to the rowing boat ahead of him, but don't tell the children."

Then it was reported from the quay that he was on his

way towards the bend. Suddenly everybody was pushing to our side of the bridge, squashing us against the rail, and it was a struggle for me and Mrs Ashcroft to hang onto the children and give them some protection. And, there he was, at the bend, moving our way. The crowd shouted.

"Don't let go of our hands, else we might lose you." I held tightly onto James and Brenda. "You know the way home, if we get split up."

Brenda suddenly jumped. "What was that?" She didn't like the water anyway, but she had heard something above us, and began to shake. "Can we go off?"

But, it was impossible to move away at that time, the crowd was pinning us to the rail and there was no escape. I reassured her that Nelson would soon be here and the crowd would return to the other side of the bridge to see him move upstream. She clung even more tightly to my hand.

Then, a man from the quay shouted something, and several of the quay workers were looking our way, and two moved to the entrance to the bridge, pointing along it, but never shouted any more. Most of the spectators were engrossed in Nelson, as he was pulled towards us with the tide, and never noticed the men pointing at the bridge again, and one moved onto the bridge to look along the deck, so I began to panic.

"Let's get off, now!"

But we couldn't move from the rail, and as much as Mrs Ashcroft pushed she could get nowhere. We had to stay put, and Brenda and James both almost squeezed my hands numb.

Suddenly, those ten seconds began, and they felt like ten minutes, as I remember a loud, metallic crack and the entire population of the bridge moved onto me, crushing me on the rails, then the crush abated. I was hitting the water, with everybody else falling on top of me. I clung tightly onto James and Brenda.

Then, nothing.

Peter Fuller's Daughter

CHAPTER 12
THREE

Salty mud filled my mouth, and my body strained, and my head panicked blindly, trying desperately to breath. I just remember nothing after that. It was as if I was dead.

Then I was being tossed around, and my lungs and stomach emptied as I was bashed on the back. I went back out.

The next thing I remember is a fat, bearded, red face looking menacingly down at me. I wanted to swing at it, but he restrained my arm. I don't remember much after that, as I went out, again.

When I did come round, I was laying in front of a roaring fire, feeling sick, sore from the crush and my sides ached as I retched, and all I could taste was the mud and salt from the river. It dawned on me what had happened.

"James! James, I'm here!" I jumped up, still retching, but was grabbed from behind.

"Calm down. You need to warm up!" The voice was not from here, with a foreign accent. It was a strange man, darker than me, with a round face and wide eyes. "Lay near the fire for a while. Please."

I didn't know what to do. Where was James?

"Where's James?" I looked around at my surroundings, and there were several people in front of the fire, wrapped in blankets and warming after the cold water, but James was not there. "Please Sir, where's James? And Brenda?"

He gently helped me back down onto the blanket. "I'll talk to Boss. I'll get him here."

The foreign man, with a far-eastern look to him, went through the front door. I looked hard at the other people, all children, but neither James nor Brenda were there. They must have been taken to another refuge. Then I noticed that one blanket was over the head of the child, so I crept over and removed it from the head. It was a dead boy, but not James.

I laid down and shivered, but, by not moving, my lungs seemed to slowly clear and my breathing became regular, but sore. Then, in a flash, my body relaxed and I was floating in some kind of trance, with absolute silence around me, with no soreness nor pain, nor retching. I was drifting in an abstract, heavenly state.

I don't know how long I had laid in front of the fire, but I was woken by the big, red, bearded face which had woken me from the river. He was smiling, seemed more friendly than before, and I strangely felt almost perfect. My chest no longer hurt, my ribs and sides never ached, and I felt so alive. I looked around and all the other children had gone.

"Three tells me you wanted someone. Who've you lost?" His voice was a soft, Yarmouth mix of kindness and authority, not as broad as many in the area, but very different to what I expected. He was a lump of a man, a bit like Dad and Joshua, but with a bit of fat about him, and looked quite rough, but spoke gently. "Shall we see if we can find your friends?"

The other children had gone, presumably collected by their families or homes, and the dead boy no longer lay there. It felt to me, at the time, like they had never been there. I began to feel it a little eerie, then I realised that we were in a pub, the serving hatch open, with some unwashed, empty mugs sitting there, and a scattering of tables and country chairs were the only furnishings. 'The man must be the landlord.' He looked like somebody who drank beer, with a slight belly and ruby cheeks. The landlord.

"Three!" The man called and the Asian man came though a side door. "I'm going out with this girl to find her friends. If any more come in, make them comfortable and warm." He grabbed my arm, helped me up, then put the blanket around my shoulders, before leading me out of the pub.

The pub wasn't right on the river, but a couple of hundred feet along towards the Acle Turnpike and was quiet, but as we left our road into the quay area, I almost fainted. The bridge was hanging down sideways, from one of its two chains, and one half was submerged in the high tide. One of the chains had broken and thrown everybody into the river, apart from a couple which had become tangled in the ironworks. Some men were climbing to release them. I could see, even from that distance, that they were not my family.

People were in the river in boats, still searching, and the death-scene had washed upriver with the tide, taking bodies quite a distance from the bridge, and my heart sank. There were people milling around, helping survivors, but there weren't many to help, just desperate families and dock workers mourning over the dead bodies layed out on the biers. Some were taking the dead bodies into the local factories and pubs. There was no screaming nor wailing, just an unhinging quiet.

I dropped to my knees, not wishing to see any more, just wanting to die.

"What's your name?" The big man crouched down with me, and took me into his arms. "Tell me your name, and we can see if we can find your family."

He was gentle, making me feel a little less alone in the World, and he so much reminded me of Dad and Joshua that my panic subsided. I opened my eyes, but never looked towards the bridge.

"I'm Eunice. Eunice Fuller." I realised that I'd gone against the Joshua's advice, and had revealed my identity, but, perhaps it wasn't too late. "I'm Eunice Ashcroft."

He continued to cuddle me, but never said anything, just sighed. After a short silence, he spoke. "Lanky Ashcroft's girl?"

I nodded, not being sure whether to be Fuller or Ashcroft. At that moment I was Ashcroft.

"Then let's find your family. Who was here?"

"Mrs Ashcroft, Stephen and Mathew, they're about nine, Brenda, who's eight, and my brother James who's eight." I felt surprisingly calm, with an air of hope that they were all right.

"Then let's check out the pubs and warehouses, where the live ones are being warmed."

We went along, past several biers (wooden stretchers), which were waiting to be taken to the pubs and factories, and we carefully checked the dead. I never knew any of them, but in the Norwich Arms we found four dead bodies, Mrs Ashcroft, Brenda, Stephen and Mathew. I finally cried.

The big man held my shoulders, then offered me a handkerchief. He was quite well groomed for a pub man, and his Yarmouth accent was very clear and deliberate, like one who had been given a good education. He so much reminded me of Dad.

"I know Lanky. I'll come with you when you go, to tell him the sad news."

"We can't go yet! James. Where's James?"

So, we worked our way around the factories and pubs, where just a handful of children remained alive and were being bathed in warm water from the brewery, but we never found James, dead nor alive. Then the big man took my hand and sat me down on a bench. He sat beside me.

"At least we haven't found him dead. There's hope yet. Shall we get out and look further? Are you ready to look that death scene in the face?"

No, I wasn't. But if I never looked it in the face, I may never find James.

His round face smiled. "When I left school I joined the Royal Navy. My last couple of years were around Canton, with the Opium War, and I saw some horrible sights, with cruelty and death becoming normal, eventually. Anyway, in my early days, during my first combat, my Petty Officer told me to look at everything, and I would soon get used to it. He was right, I became immune to the trauma. So, will you go out and look at everything out there? It'll help you to accept it."

I didn't want to, but he seemed like *my* Petty Officer, mentoring me in this awful moment of life and death. I agreed, and he led me outside.

I looked hard, with my mentor holding tightly onto my arm, giving me courage, and it was the worst sight I had ever seen, not the dead ones being retrieved, but the living ones hurting. I remember Dad telling me that when we die we go to heaven, released from this life, and those left behind are the ones left to suffer the loss. I began to realise what my dad was teaching me, survival through having a thick skin, and I was able to look at all this suffering without even a tear. I felt a tinge of shame.

"Look over there." He pointed to the other side of the river, but I was distracted by something trivial.

"Sir, what's your name?" I don't even know why it mattered, but I had to know. "Please, Sir, I'd like to know your name."

He looked down at me and gave me a warm smile. "Luke. Luke Smith. Now, Eunice, look over there. They're putting a net across the river. The tide will be turning soon, so the bodies will either become laid out on the mud upriver, or'll be washed down with the tide and out to sea. So, the net'll catch those being washed away. We'll find James, if he's in the river. Promise."

They had removed the bodies from the stricken bridge, and, upriver, boats were sculling in all directions, some scanning the bottom of the river with boathooks, but all keeping deathly silent. It was what I remembered most about the scene, the silence. It was like a morgue.

"Sir," I suddenly recalled calling Joshua Sir, "sorry, Luke, what if James has walked home? He knows the way."

So, Luke nodded and suggested that we walk there, to find out, but I couldn't bring myself to face Lanky. He delivered me back to the pub, and walked to the vicarage alone, suggesting that it would be for the best, since he seemed to know Lanky quite well.

"Will you bring him back here, if he's there?" I made a decision that our plan was still on the cards, to get out of the vicarage and away from Lanky, and the awful events of that day would be the catalyst for that new life. I prayed that it would be both me and James leaving.

"If I bring him back here...." He stopped dead. "Let's take it on step at a time."

I never knew quite what he meant, and he left before I could ask.

Anyway, Luke left me with Three, who sat me in front of the fire and made some food. He was so kind, but almost sickeningly servient with his devotion to me as he shuffled and skuttled about. I felt I should talk to him, being careful not to talk down to him in any way, especially as he may not have been able to talk good English.

"Sir, what's your name?"

He stood more upright and smiled. "I'm Three. You've heard Boss call me."

"Yes, but is that your real name?"

"Of course it is." He had a better command of the English language than I had first thought. He had a very round face, quite dark, but not the slit eyes of the Chinese; they were very rounded. "Three is my christian name. You can call me Three, not Sir. And, Your Ladyship, what should I call you?"

"Anything but Your Ladyship! I *hate* Lady Maybush, and want no association with her type, thank you very much. So, anything but Your Ladyship!" I huffed.

"Calm down, Wench. Would that be better? Is that the best name for you, Wench?" He began laughing, and the moment lightened. "I'll call you Wench, unless you tell me otherwise." He was very sweet, then he went to the door to let a couple of ladies in, who were there to thank him for looking after their children. It was a beautiful moment, seeing their faces as they shook his hand. It gave me some hope for James.

Three sat beside me and pointed at the bread and dripping. "You need to eat that, it'll give you energy and the beer will keep you hydrated. When I was on-board it kept us alive, so, eat and drink, Wench." He was as far away from servient as was possible. He completely relaxed me, reminding me of the red squirrel which just got on with his life, no matter what.

I was beginning to feel like a hard, thick-skinned survivor, not shedding tears for James, nor Brenda, but being prodded by my earlier view of those people left to suffer the loss of the dead children from the bridge, and I began to think more about the living; Mum and Cordelia. I just needed to look at Three to feel alive.

"Three, my name's Eunice. Please call me Eunice."

"I know, Boss said to look after the children, especially Eunice. So, with your permission, I'll call you Eunice, not Wench. Boss said you're a special friend, important."

Strange! How would I be so important to Luke Smith? Then I remembered my mistake, telling him that I'm Eunice Fuller. He clearly took that one in. He knew that I wasn't Ashcroft.

"Did he say anything else about me?"

He shook his head, but as he was about to go into the kitchen, he stopped and looked carefully at me. "I think he likes you a lot. He's lost his wife, and is lonely. He's a good man. We're all good people in here." He was going to say something else, but stopped himself. "You'll fit in here."

Was this going to be another Lanky Ashcroft? I tried not to think about it, and concentrate on my current concerns, like, do I still have a brother? Then, will I ever see Mum and Cordelia? Then, where the hell am I, and why?

Peter Fuller's Daughter

CHAPTER 13
SHAME

I waited in front of the fire as Luke visited Lanky. Every time I tried to do something, such as put some logs on the fire, Three was there, like a loyal retriever who wanted only to please his master, and I wasn't sure if that was me or Luke, but I appreciated the attention. I had begun to feel some shock waves, and my hands would shake every time I tried to do anything, so, Three gave me a glass of milk laced with whisky.

Then, the front door was banging.

"Go away, we're closed! No beer today, go to the others if they're serving!" Three stood in front of the door, very upright, ready for anything, and in charge. "Boss says we're closed, so we're closed!"

For a little, far-eastern man, he certainly had some balls. He rather cockily sat down with me by the fire.

"Boss said not to open, so I won't, and besides, Mary can't be here, she's with her family. She lost a cousin in the river." He suddenly grinned into my face. "If we do open, you'll have to be the real wench while she's away, do her job."

"Job? What's that?"

"The serving wench. But Boss would kill me if I allowed that. You're a special guest, so getting groped by the drinkers would get me hung, drawn and quartered. I'd rather fight them as they try to get in than have to face Boss."

Then the door was banging. He jumped over and stood in front of the door. "We're closed! Go away, I ain't joking!"

The drinkers went elsewhere.

"What if they'd tried to get in? Would you have served them?"

"Me? I'm Three, and my father, One, taught me well. I'd have put them back out that door. Believe you me, straight out the door. They're fishermen, not fighters."

Three was beginning to intrigue me, but before we went any further into his past and present, the door was again banging.

"Go away, we're closed!"

"It's me!"

Three jumped up and let the caller in. It was Luke. He smiled at Three, who immediately went into the back, then he sat on a windsor chair, close to me.

"Sorry, but James hasn't shown." He dropped his head. "In case, I stopped at the Police Station and asked them to look out for him, and send him here if he shows. I thought carefully about it all, so I told them not to send him back to the vicarage, he wouldn't be safe." He hung his head and thought carefully about how to explain things, but eventually he breathed deeply. "There's a lot that I ought to tell you, but for now, I'll just say that he blames you for all of this, and says good riddance. The man's a lunatic, stripped of sense by the laudanum and whisky. His next move will probably be the town's nut house."

Why would he blame me? That's insanity, and perhaps he *should* have been in the lunatic asylum. But, that wasn't important, what was, was that James wasn't there. I felt light-headed from the shock of the day and the whisky, but now I felt sick. I had that feeling of suspension, swinging in a vacuum, upside-down and my blood rushing to my head, unable to get one way nor the other, and not knowing if James was dead or alive. How can I go anywhere without knowing? How could I go anywhere, at all, with or without him? I had a horrible gut feeling that life was not exactly what it seemed. Perhaps the time under water, unconscious, was playing with my brain.

"Eunice. I know it would be better to know one way or the other, and you will soon. When the tide goes right out, he'll either be on the mud, or in the net, then you'll know. In the meantime, you need to get some rest, you're shaking.

Three! Get some hot milk for Eunice!"

Three made up a bed for me by the fire and I slept like a log.

It was just getting light when I awoke, and I could hear a lot of noise coming from the river area, but could not see the river from the window. I sat by the fire, which had gone out, and waited for Luke and Three to arise. They were soon bashing around in the pub, arranging the furniture in readiness for the customers. Luke couldn't afford to remain closed for a second day, and it was Saturday, their busiest day.

"Good morning Eunice!" Three folded my bedding up, then took it to the back room. "We're opening today, so you best come into the back. Some of these fishermen and dockers can get very abusive after a couple of ales. They get frustrated, and say that the only thing they get out at sea is the giant skate, you know, the mermaids."

"What do you mean?" I was confused. "What do the skate and mermaids do?"

Suddenly, I could see Three's face redding up, and he scuttled out to the back room. I followed him. It was the kitchen and servery, with a range, a hatch through to the bar, and steps down from one corner to the cellar. In the other corner there were steps up to the first floor.

"Mary should be in soon, so you don't need to be the wench. You can be Her Ladyship." Three giggled to himself. "You can't go out to the bar, Boss said. Not yet, anyway."

Luke had gone out to find out what would happen to his beer and spirit delivery.

"Bridge has gone, and they've already begun removing it from the river, to let the boat traffic through, but our problem is the beer delivery. We're this side of the river, and the brewers are the other side, in Yarmouth. Our beer always came over the bridge!"

His beer would have to be ferried over the river, but that wasn't my concern. At that moment my head swung right back to reality, James.

"I need to look for James!"

Three stopped what he was doing, and hung his head. "Boss said you must stay here, until he's back. I have to stop you going out."

"But James...."

"He's out there looking. Once he's been to the whisky maker, he'll see what's happening with the search." He was apologetic. "Please don't go out, I'd have to stop you. Don't know how."

It seems he would have laid out yesterday's drinkers if they had pushed through the door, but he didn't seem to know how to stop me. What was he afraid of? In my fuzzied head, I felt like a highly honoured prisoner, and I had no idea why, so, I sat in the corner until Mary arrived. She had lost a cousin in the disaster, but managed to get on with life from the start, as we all had to. She showed me the cellar, which had another stairway up to the outside of the pub, with a hatch over it. She unlocked the hatch, expecting a delivery of beer. She also showed me around the tiny kitchen, where she made sandwiches for the customers, and spoke briefly about the men and their hands, but really said little else. She was very quiet, and very ordinary looking, and probably thick-skinned, putting up with the drinkers' hands. Being thick-skinned was part of her job as the bar wench, and that intrigued me.

Then Luke came through the front door.

"Right Three, our delivery's coming, but on a hand cart across the ferry, so it may not be the full delivery. Have to make do, stick a bit of water in to stretch it out, but not too much. Don't want to end up in the jail." He gave Mary a supporting cuddle, then turned his attention to me. His large frame stood in front of me, obscuring the light from the window, and sighed. "We need to get out there and check the bodies. They've collected a load from upstream, and took some from the net, so you need to identify James, if he's there. Are you all right to do it?"

I had to be. I needed to know if I still had a brother, so he took my arm, led me outside, down the short street to the river-front, and there it was, the stricken bridge. Engineers were all over it, removing it from the busy waterway, and destroying the evidence of the fateful day. Soon it would all be forgotten about, apart from the funerals, memories and the legal cases, and good riddance. It was a crime of social justice to have allowed so many people onto such a poorly designed and built bridge, and I could feel myself developing a hatred for it all. Yes, I hated the very thought of Yarmouth suspension bridge and all that it stood for, and thank God the railway would soon be making its mark on Yarmouth, and building a new, substantial bridge across the Bure. If only we had respected Brenda enough to watch from the quay. It wasn't just the bridge that I was beginning to hate, it was also me. What had I done?

We had to go across on the ferry to get to the brewery, where the last of the bodies had been laid. The little bit of time getting there helped to settle me, and I arrived clear-headed. The job had to be done.

Luke held my hand as we were shown along the line of bodies, mostly children, but I never found James. The Devil must have been looking down at me as I inwardly cursed at not finding him, and I suddenly felt so ashamed of myself. I should have been pleased that he wasn't one of the dead, but instead I felt annoyed. I just burst into tears.

Luke held me tightly as I wept.

"Come on, let's get home."

But, before he took me home, he spoke to the men in the brewery, explaining about James being missing, and if he was to turn up, to take him to the Vauxhall Room, *not* to the Vicarage. They were all very pleased to help wherever they could. It was a small community, and when the shit hit, they were all in the same boat. They also promised to let him know if any more bodies turned up.

After spending some time watching the engineers

dismantling, and the small boats squeezing past the wreckage in an effort to get on with life, we went 'home'.

CHAPTER 14
ME?

The pub was noisy and frightening by the time we arrived back, 'home' as Luke called it, and it took my mind off my feeling of utter shame. You see, when I never found James in the line of dead, I was so disappointed, and I was reeling from that shame in that I had *wanted* to find him dead. Not finding his body meant that he could still be alive, and I should have been celebrating, not cursing. Could I spend my whole life searching, wondering if I had killed him or if I'd just lost him? I'd never felt so confused in my life.

But, the bar brought me back down to earth.

Poor Mary, the wench, showed me how to stand up to life and get on with it. As she served four beers to a table of fishermen, one of them grabbed hold of her breast, and she swung the tray straight in his face. It looked like he was about to hit her back, but the rest of the bar cheered her, defusing the man's pride. He just hid his face. But, I also noticed that Three was standing by the hatch, ready for action. I began to think that Three was more than just a barman. And, the customers clearly respected him and Luke to the point of nodding their heads, in lieu of doffing their caps which lay on the tables.

Luke ordered me, quite bluntly, to stay in the back. I could understand why Three called him Boss.

Once the hustle and bustle of the opening hours was past, I sat in front of the fire with Three.

"Is it always so aggressive?" I asked Three carefully, looking into his face as we spoke, just as Dad had taught me. "Poor Mary has to fight them off. Some of them, anyway."

"Today was normal. As long as they just grab her, and don't hit her back, she's all right with it. It's her job, and she doesn't want to work in the fish factories. When she was a little girl she used to help her family on the beach, gutting the herring and mackerel as they come off the boats, and filleting, and mending lines and nets. She said that her hands were completely numb some days, bleeding others days, especially in the winter. This is easy for her."

"What if they do go too far?"

"Then, they get a wack, and straight out the door. They all know."

I kept his face in my mind as we spoke. He wasn't bragging, nor exaggerating, I could tell by his expressions, and he was clearly used to violence.

He continued, "We don't get many fights in here, not bad ones. People die fighting, and these just want a few drinks before going back out to sea. They're a good crowd. They look after each other, and Mary, and so do we. Me and Boss."

"Have you known Luke for long?"

"A few years. It's a long story, one for another day. Now, today is about you. What will you do now?"

"How do you mean? I'll look for James."

"Well, he wasn't on the mud, nor in the net, so he's either missed the net, or he was pulled out, alive. What will you do now?"

I wish I could have just forgotten all about it, as the red squirrel would have done, and go forward, but that probably wasn't going to happen for a while. I needed to face it.

"I don't know. I wish Joshua was here, he would help me. But he's miles south, in Blythburgh. In heaven, home."

Three pulled me in for a hug.

"Now, Her Ladyship, Joshua isn't here, but me and Boss are. And Mary. So, you're not alone, and since you're so special to Boss, we'll do whatever we can for you. You're not alone. Not here, in *our* heaven."

He stopped, then got to his feet and put some logs onto the fire. It was a habit, tending the fire in front of you, since it was May and warming up for the summer. But we sat in front of it anyway, enjoying the soothing flicker and the smell of carbon, and it reminded me of home, with Mum and James, and the older memories of Dad and the little ones, and right then I had nobody. Well, I had Three and Luke. That's more than Mum's got. Then I wondered what James would have, if he was still alive.

"What if James is looking for me? We're the wrong side of the river for the vicarage, so he may never find me."

"Boss has spoken to many people, and they'll look out for him. He'll not get away. And besides, they'll not cross James...." He stopped dead, then smiled into my face. "What's your name?"

What a strange question, a complete change of direction. I had already told Luke what my name was. Mind you, I did slip up, and I began to wonder if I'd made a big mistake in even mentioning Fuller, but I didn't think that he had noticed. "It's Eunice Ashcroft. You know it is."

"Yes, I know. But nobody believes it, especially Boss. He thinks you're somebody very special to him, from the past. An incarnation of somebody very special. And lots of other people think the same. Or very similar."

I wished that Joshua was here, not just to look after me, but to scold me for being so stupid. But, at the time, I had just been pulled out of the river, and was filled with salty water and mud, so perhaps he would forgive me. 'I hope he answers my letter soon.'

"What are you getting at? Am I in danger?"

"Oh no! Never in danger, no no, no. Quite the opposite. This is Yarmouth, and Peter Fuller's name is written in the stars, a living legend. You'll never be in danger in Yarmouth, not with everybody knowing. Eunice Fuller, and her missing brother, James Fuller. The children of Peter Fuller." He laughed. "Whatever that means. I never heard of him!"

I didn't know what to say. All I knew about my dad was what Joshua had told me. He was a fighter and banned from coming to Norfolk by the Sheriff of Suffolk, and was in hiding as my dad, in Blythburgh. Legend? I was led to believe that it wasn't even safe for him to come to Norfolk, and I should never reveal who I am, and should keep my opinionated mouth shut, or else.... I was reeling over Joshua's advice, but intrigued to know what my father really was, apart from a fighter. Should I keep my mouth shut, or not?

"That's ridiculous! I'm Eunice Ashcroft, and my auntie, who looked after me and James, was drowned. My uncle, Lanky, doesn't want me, so I 'm here. Eunice....Ashcroft!"

He put his hands in the air, and shouted, "Then, pleased to meet you, Eunice Ashcroft! Welcome to our home!" He shook my hand, for some reason, probably as a joke since he never believed a word of it. "You'll always be safe with us. This is our World, whoever you are!"

He shuffled into the back to start preparing for the next day.

CHAPTER 15
THE LEGEND OF PETER FULLER

Luke had been upstairs, preparing a bedroom for me. It was all very basic with a bed and a tallboy, and very much what I was used to, with a potty under the bed. The pub used to rent rooms out, so there were several rooms available, but the one he had given me had a nice window which looked out of the side of the building, towards the river. I shivered as I looked out; I could just see the stricken bridge. I made a mental note of that, to make sure I didn't look.

I also made a mental note that Luke wasn't expecting me to go anywhere soon, he had given me a bedroom. But that was a pleasant feeling, since I trusted him and Three, and the intrigue of why he held me in such esteem, as a virtual prisoner, kept my mind from the foul thoughts of what poor James might be going through, if he's still alive. I silently said a prayer.

I was sure that the landlord's special thoughts for me were not just about my pretty looks and sleek figure, but I was at the age when it wouldn't have been a bad thing if it had been the case. He was older than me, a bit fat, but kind, with property. If Cordelia had been here she would have been pushing me forwards, with an aim for us both being set up, me marrying the suitor and her being my personal maid-in-waiting. Yes, Luke was an attractive beau, fat but attractive.

The next day was Sunday, but I asked Luke if I could stay away from the church, in case I bumped into Lanky. He didn't think it likely, as they used a different church, but he was happy for me to stay with Three, who was a non-practicing Buddhist. I decided to help with the preparations for the twelve o'clock opening.

I was put with Mary, scrubbing the pine table-tops.

I had to ask, "Mary, you know all about the fishing....

Three said that the men only got the skate, or the mermaids, when out at sea. What did he mean?"

She laughed, then looked around, and in her slow Yarmouth accent explained, "It's only myth, I think, cos the skate ain't that big around here, but Three's probably thinking of his navy days, when they got big skates, and hung them up to use. You know, thingmy them." She looked at me like I was a schoolchild. "You know, with their things, cos they're like a girl's. And they call them mermaids."

Suddenly I realised what she was saying, and turned beetroot. I never asked any more, just scrubbed the tables and thought about grown men doing *that* to a fish, even if it was called a mermaid.

Mary wasn't going to start a new conversation, so I had to do it. "Do you know who I am? Everybody else thinks they do."

"I do. You're the girl of the fighter, Fuller. My dad knows about his famous fight, and he'd like to meet him, and shake his hand. He killed the most famous gypsy fighter ever, and now your dad is the most famous. You are her, aren't you?"

"If I was, would I be safe? You know, people getting their own back, and that sort of thing?"

"I think so. But I only know what my dad told me last night about the fight. So I don't really know, but Boss'll look after you if you're not. And Three. And the customers. We all look after each other over this side of the river. Don't know about the other side, but I think you'll still be all right over there. With the bridge gone, not many will be over here for drinks. It'll keep our Worlds on the proper sides, if you know what I mean."

"No, I'm not sure what you mean."

"Oh." She breathed heavily. "Well, they're them, and we're us. That's all."

I still didn't know what she meant, but she wouldn't talk any more about it, just saying, "Ask Boss."

It seemed that, since the railway had opened the previous

year, business on this side of the river was booming. Much of the cart traffic which went across the suspension bridge, onto the Acle Turnpike to Norwich, had already slowed with the option of the railway, but with both the rail and road traffic the Vauxhall side of the river was booming. So was Luke's pub. But, now that the bridge was gone, things would surely change. My young lady brain began to wonder if it would make Luke a more attractive catch, or just a bankrupt.

"My dad said last night, that they'll have to make another bridge quickly, else the railway is cut off from Yarmouth." She was very quiet, slow, but never stupid. I liked her. "Hopefully they'll come over the ferry for drinks, and Boss said that we're getting more train workers in for drinks. Not just fishermen and tanners. We should be all right for jobs. You gonna work here?"

My head wasn't too sure what I was going to do. I could stay until I've found James, but then what? I know what I'd like to do, get Mum and Cordelia out from the workhouse, but how? My mind was swilling around all over the place, but was just beginning to realise just how fortunate I had been. It was rumoured that more than eighty people had drowned in the accident, and I didn't *think* that I was one of them. I had to pinch myself to make sure, but that wasn't conclusive.

"You know, Eunice, that hardly any were taken out alive. Just a couple of handfuls. You'll have to live for all your family. You know, Three and Boss lost all their families over the years, so they know what it's like. I'm lucky, I still talk with my mum and dad. We're lucky over this side, one big family. Helps that we don't live in the rows over there, where they all get diseased, but this side of the river is better and cleaner. You'll like it here." She talked a lot more than I first realised, so I let her carry on. I was learning from her.

Once she had stopped filling me in about our side of the river and theirs, I felt I had to tell her something. "You know you said your dad would like to shake my dad's hand, well perhaps you should tell him that he won't be able to. My dad's dead."

"It's all right. So's mine."

She smiled at me, opened the front doors as some drinkers had turned up, and I went out to the back room. I pondered over my life, and what the hell was happening to it, and right through the session, as I made the sandwiches, I felt more and more confused.

When I found the opportunity to talk to Luke, he was very keen to talk about his past, and mine. I never asked him about this side and the other side, as I thought he might think that I'm being silly, with such a silly question. I began to wonder what the question even meant.

"I was a young man when the big fight was rumoured, between Romany Joe and a bloke from Suffolk, and all the odds were in favour of the gypsy, Romany Joe Taylor, who was a big name in the sport. But I had this inkling that something was going to go against the odds, and that the man from Suffolk would win. I looked into it, and could get odds of twelve to one for the Suffolk mush. So, I spoke to Mum and Dad, who were landlords of this pub, but Dad didn't want to know, he had his own problems. Now, his problem was the owner of the building, who wanted to sell out, and wanted five hundred pounds. Mum and Dad never had that sort of money, nor did I. I was just fifteen, but wanted to take over the business when they retired, and it was looking bleak. All Dad wanted me to do was become a commissioned officer in the Navy, as I was bright enough and he'd made sure I got a good education locally, but it wasn't what I wanted. I wanted to run the pub when they'd had enough, or with them before that, and it looked like we were going to be thrown out. So I spoke to Dad again about the fight. A fifty pound bet would buy us the pub, with six hundred and fifty pounds back, for fifty pounds stake. That's what we'd win if the Suffolk fighter won. Now, after a lot of soul searching, Dad agreed that we would be thrown out of the pub if we didn't bet, thrown out if we did bet and lose, but could buy the pub if we won. One in three chance of getting the pub, so he agreed that we would do it. We put fifty pounds, our entire wealth, on the Suffolk fighter. We put fifty pounds on Reed."

Suddenly I was wondering about Joshua, Joshua Reed, the man who Dad said was the best fighter.

"Johua Reed?"

"If that was his name, I only knew his as Reed from Suffolk. Anyway, the fight was all set to take place, then something happened to Reed, and had to call it off. There was trouble, believe you me, as all the arrangements, the bets, the bribes down the police station, it was all for nothing. There was going to be murder. Then Reed's stand-in agreed to the fight. The bookies and sponsors all agreed and it went ahead. Your dad, Peter Fuller, had the fight, in place of Reed. I was worried about my bet, and thought about withdrawing it, but the maths still showed us being kicked out if anything but a win for the Suffolk fighter transpired. No bet, no pub. Me and Dad warily left the bet with the bookie." He took a breather.

He looked into my face. "Have you ever been to one of your Dad's fights?"

"I don't think he ever fought again. Not that type of fight, just with the poachers. And all he ever said to me was that his mate was the best fighter."

A grin spread over his face, before continuing. "On the day, your dad was the best in the World. Anyway, knuckle-fighting's not for the faint-hearted. You have to be standing to stay in the fight, no biting, kicking or gouging, and no wrestling. Bare knuckles, and elbows and heads, until one or other is down, and stays down. They beat each other almost senseless, rupturing their insides, pulverising their brains, until one final blow did it. One was just about standing, the other looked like he was dead. Peter Fuller was the one standing, the champion of all champions, and an absolute legend, a hero.

"The whole field began to get uneasy as the gypsies began to curse the result, so, we decided to get out quickly, but when I found the bookie, Dad was scared to ask for our money, it was a big sum, six hundred and fifty pounds, but when I asked, the bookie shook my hand and said 'thank you'. He had taken so much money on the gypsy, that if Romany Joe had won, he never would have been able to pay out, he would be bankrupted, and probably killed. So, he was the happiest bookie alive that day, and we were the happiest pub owners. That bookie and us, well we owe everything we have to your dad's fight. *Everything*. He's a living legend in these parts." He raised his eyebrows. "The gypsies might not see it that way, but...."

That explained the legend. It also explained his admiration for me, and why he felt he owes me something, and also explained why Joshua Reed felt he owed Peter's children something. It explained a lot to me. Perhaps I should have explained to Luke that Peter Fuller, the living legend, was dead. But, when I had told Mary, she just confused me with her response, so I never risked telling Luke.

CHAPTER 16
THE OPIUM WARS

I suppose that was sufficient to make him think a lot of me, and I hoped that it wasn't the only reason he liked me, after all, Cordelia always said that I was pretty enough and intelligent enough to attract any man. But what was there to attract me to him, apart from his property and a business which could be destroyed by the bridge disaster?

"Now, what about you? Why aren't you married?"

He looked at me as if I shouldn't have been asking, but nodded and answered. "Yes, I was married. My wife died soon after our wedding. Influenza."

"Sorry. I suppose I need to tell you that my dad died of influenza, just a few months ago. The living legend is now a proper legend."

"Sorry to hear that, also. It's a fact of life, death. We all have to get used to it, sadly, then we all have to believe that it's Gods will. Do you believe in that?"

"No, never. God explains a lot that we can't explain ourselves, but death? Why would God be in charge of death? If he is, then I hate him for doing that to the bridge."

He smiled, in thought. "You know, death isn't so bad, once you get used to it."

I thought he was talking about the looking-it-in-the-face, as his Petty Officer had taught him.

"Anyway, I think it was the designers and the engineers, and blacksmiths, who you need to blame." He carried on smiling , but continued after a nod of the head, "The fight. It changed my life. Now, your dad was taken away, in a real state, and the other fighter, the gypsy, was taken away on a bier, and died later, but Peter Fuller *must* have recovered, he had you." He looked at me in a similar way to how Lanky used to look at me, but with a feeling of love, not just lust.

"He survived to leave an incarnation of his spirit."

I was enjoying the compliments, and I think it was all a bit of a flirt, but I knew nothing about him, so I asked about *his* past, not mine. What had he done all his life? It seemed to matter to me.

"Right, mine. Yes, with the winnings from the fight, we bought the pub, our home, and I helped to run it and maintain it, then married a local girl. She was lovely, same age as me, sixteen, called Jane. Within weeks of our wedding, she died." He took a few moments out to reflect. "It hit me so hard.... In the end, I did what Dad had always wanted me to do, I joined the Navy. He insisted that I get a commission, as I had the education, but I didn't want to tie myself into it for too long, so I just enlisted. Signed up for three years. I got so bored on ship, went across to the West Indies, then down along the coast of South America, and round into the Pacific. It was a real adventure, saw some action on the way, and it always sounds so romantic, but boring. You wouldn't believe how boring it can be out at sea. I had to find something to keep me sane, so, as a big lad with an active mind, I got myself really involved, and to cut a long story short, by the time the Opium War was on, I'd worked my way up to Warrant Officer, and on my way to that commission that Dad always wanted for me. I'd become a navy man, through and through.

"Then, must've been during thirty-nine, we ended up in Canton. We were fighting the Chinese, who had banned the sale and dealing of Opium for anything but medicinal uses, and putting anyone to death who broke the new rules, so Britain was at war with the Chinese, to protect their opium trades, which ultimately gave them the money to pay for the tea which was becoming a boom industry."

He stretched his arms up behind his head. "So much cruelty. Couldn't believe how cruel people are to each other, on both sides. Saw it in other places, but not on this scale. And I was in charge of the landing crew, so we saw the streets with dead bodies, with children strung up, and then the affects of the opium. I could understand why the chinks wanted to stop the recreational use of opium, millions were slowly dying from it. Millions and millions.

"Anyway, you don't want to hear the shit side of it all, and I don't want to remember it. So, moving on, there was this bloke who came to the ship and wanted to join up, to fight the Chinese. His family had moved to Canton for work, from the Mã River, and had got caught up in the executions, and he was the only one of his family not around when it happened, the only one not killed, so he wanted to kill the chinks even more than we did. It was Three. He really wanted his revenge. The Captain wasn't sure, but I'd lost a couple of men on our expeditions, so he agreed that he could come into my team, and he was really good. He can speak good French, which was useful, and he could fight. He still can, his dad was a fighter who took on mentored youngsters, and his son was one of them. It seems to be a bit of a religious thing with the Buddhists, called martial arts. Three became my right-hand man, right until the end in forty three, and we both left together. As you can guess, he's been with me ever since, and will probably be with me forever."

"I thought you were to be commissioned. What happened?" I noticed that his face was a little blank, so, I asked again. "What happened? Why weren't you commissioned?

He shook his head several times, and then took a massive breath. "Just never happened. Never." He looked me in the eye, and I'm sure he had tear in his. "Shouldn't really tell you, but I think it'd be all right to talk about it, if I'm careful."

He sat upright and breathed deeply for a couple of minutes, to compose himself, but his face went even redder as his head became overdosed with oxygen. I thought he was about to go out.

"Wake up!" I shook his arm. "Stop breathing or you'll faint."

He held his breath for half a minute, and the oxygen-rush subsided. He relaxed.

"Sorry." He settled down beside me and began. "I went inland with Three and the rest of my team, to locate a French general who had been taken captive, because we were told that he was important. I'll never forget the thoughts which rushed through my head when we were told that this man was so important, because, when I looked around at my team, I realised that I was looking at the most important people in the Royal Navy; us. But we had orders to go and die for this frog. Why did we do it? Blindly follow our superiors, that's why." He sat silently in thought for a long couple of minutes. "Well, we did as we were told, for our Queen and Country, obediently walking into death. Why?"

He looked me in the eye and was expecting me to tell him why he did it. At that point I didn't really know what he had even done, let alone why.

So, he continued. "According to our intelligence, the frog was being held in a small village, north of Canton, about two days walk, and so we set off in earnest. We had ample powder and shot for our Brunswicks, and being twenty-strong, we felt confident. The locals were always suspicious of us, but never interfered, and we made good progress towards our destination, until we settled in for the night, a little way south of the village. As the night turned pitch black, the guard overpowered an intruder, and he was alone and un-armed, so I interrogated him, using whatever persuasion I needed, and he talked, admitting that he was a seller of opium, for illegal purposes, which kind-of made him one of us, in dispute with the Chinese over the banning of recreational use of opium. He was an ally, and we untied him. Anyway, Three asked him if he knew of the French general, and he gingerly told us that he was dead. What do you do, in such a situation? If we'd gone back and reported that we were too late, then the bloody frog had turned up, we would've been hung, so we needed to confirm the dealer's story. We needed to see the body. There was no point in us all going, so I made the decision to go myself, the dealer agreed to take me through the dark, and he confirmed that we could be there and back in a couple of hours. I set off behind the Chinese man."

Luke looked around the pub, at nothing, just clearing his mind a little.

"The little chink was himself a marked man, as a dealer, with a death penalty hanging over his head, and I could see how he had survived for so long. He moved with absolute stealth, in total silence, and was part of the night. I just about managed to match his invisible presence, and after about an hour, we arrived at the village. I was very conspicuous in my navy jacket and trousers, towering head-and-shoulders above the locals, and so the dealer crept into one of the houses close to where the body was, then returned, indicating that we had permission to hide in the house. From there we would be able to see the body. Despite my reservations, I had to trust the man, and so crept in behind him.

"The Cantonese family were all sitting on the ground around a very low table, having just eaten, and the woman of the house invited me to eat some with them. In the flickering light I took a small bowl of soup. Then the man of the house went to the door and beckoned me over. From there, I could see the general, in the flickering light from some torches. He was tied to a post, hands behind the post and head securely strapped to keep it upright, with his gaze forwards. The entire front of his body had been skinned, his penis and genitals cut partly through, to leave them hanging, and part of his intestines pulled out from a cut in his stomach. They called it Lingchi."

He turned his nose up. "I'd become immune to the trauma of seeing such acts but the lady of the house was quite upset about it all, and refused to even look. Apparently, the executioner was a highly respected craftsman, administering the General his punishment for about three hours before the poor man was allowed to pass out. I'll never forget that satisfied smile on the dead man's face. He had finally escaped his torture.

"I was satisfied that the general was well and truly dead, and would not turn up to embarrass us, so the dealer agreed to lead me back to my team. He was a superb gorilla, a survivor, and we were soon approaching our camp."

Luke stopped to reflect on his memories of the dealer. "Yes, superb. Him and Three would have made a dangerous team. Anyway, as we approached, shouting came through the darkness. It was from the camp, and the dealer stopped dead. He beckoned me to follow, we took a broad detour of the camp, and approached from the other side. We could see through the scrub. The area was lit up with torches, and my team were either on the ground, or strung up." A tear appeared in his eye, and stuttered as he said, "Three was strung up. Two were strung up, all the others lay on the ground, dead, with the camp surrounded by Chinese soldiers. Three and 'The Ferryman' hung on the posts. I'll never forget that feeling in my heart." He had a good sniff. "Anyway, the dealer held tightly onto my arm, then pulled me to leave."

Luke sat pondering and shaking his head, and the tears slowly ran down his cheeks. I never pushed him to carry on, and it felt like a lifetime as I waited for him to say something. Then, he suddenly shook his head and pulled himself out of it. He smiled.

"Life. Sometimes it's not the best thing to reflect on. Some of it, anyway. You know, Eunice, we're taught in the navy that choices sometimes have to made, and one of the choices is whether or not it's your turn to go. You don't always get to make the choice, but at the time I did get to choose, and was driven by what my PO had taught me. 'If you can't save the others, save yourself. You're no use to the navy dead.' Three and The Ferryman were on the posts. I knew what was going to happen to them, they were to end up with a smile on their faces, and mutilated bodies, but I couldn't save them. All I could do was to help them, but I knew I couldn't save them. I stopped the dealer from pulling me along, and made my choice."

He abruptly stood up and left the room.

With questions flying around in my head like a gaggle of panicked geese, I set about my table scrubbing.

Mary had kept well away while we discussed Luke's past, but came over once he had left. I expected her to tell me more, but, "He'll tell you in his own time. He has to be careful right now, but he'll tell you, I promise."

I scrubbed a couple of tables, before Luke returned.

He led me to a private corner, well away from Mary, and we sat as opposites at the table.

"So, here I am."

I could see that. I was almost becoming immune to the confusion, so, I joined with the theme of utter confusion, often called beer-talk, or bollicks, despite both being sober! "I can see that you're here. I can feel it, I can feel you. And I know that I'm here, but where is 'here'? If you're here, and I'm here, where are we?"

He laughed, took a glance towards Mary, then put his hand onto mine. "We're home. The Vauxhall Room, in Vauxhall. Home. And it's your home, if you want it. The others have both agreed, and you're welcome to become one of us. Here, in our home."

Suddenly, I came back down to earth. Was this a proposal of marriage? If so, it was the coldest, least convincing proposal I could ever imagine. "Now that's enough of your games! I'm not staying here as one of your team, Warrant Officer. We're not in the bloody navy now, so don't even *try* to enlist me. I ain't signing up for that!" I huffed, and considered going to my room, but I could feel Mary's eyes on me, holding me in the seat. "You still haven't told me why you're here. You worked towards that commission, and you're *here*, as you've been kind enough to point out. So, moving on from where, why? Why you here?"

"All right, I owe you an explanation. Well, when we got

back to Portsmouth, I was expecting a commission, but there was such a glut of military men, since the end of the Napoleonic Wars, that they offered me a permanent Warrant Office rank, or I could leave. I.... well, I'm not in the navy, now." He nodded in thought. "I thought about going with the East India Company, but after careful thought, especially about Mum and Dad, I ended up back here. They both died before I got back. So, here I am, a landlord with my own pub, and security of the property, and on my own."

He smiled at me as if to say 'well?' Well what? I had just lost the rest of my family, and was wary of taking on a new one with somebody so old, and with a record of past violence, and no children. He may not even be fertile. But, he was kind, gentle, with security. Perhaps. But why was Three here? He couldn't save Three from the post, and here we are, all of us. I felt that he never wanted to talk about that bit, and he wasn't convincing about his demob, so I asked, "Tell me some more about yourself. Please."

"Not sure what else to tell. Once I'd worked it all out, I accepted it. Now, I'm thirty-three, bored with being alone, and want to share what I have with a loved one, and have children, maybe, but mostly I want to share my existence."

It was sounding a tiny bit more like a proposal of love, rather than duty.

I waited for more, like *what* he had worked out, or even *who* he wanted to share his life with, but he just seemed frozen to his seat. This, a man who would kill you if he needed to, surely wasn't afraid of me. If the men in the bar want Mary's tit, they just grab them, until she whacks them, so if he wants me, why can't he just grab me, why can't he say? It's not hard, surely, and it's not my place to make the move, I'm a lady.

But he made no more moves, just carefully stood up and went out of the room to the bar.

CHAPTER 17
GUILT

That night, I had a vision in my sleep, some might call it a nightmare.

I awoke screaming, and suddenly Three was there, followed by Luke with his Warrant Officer's sword in hand. As Three checked the tiny room, Luke sat on the bed, taking me into his arms as I sobbed my heart out. He never asked any questions.

From that moment I was in mourning. James was dead, never to return from his watery world, and it was my fault. I knew what I had done, and wondered how I could live with myself. Any hope that had lingered in my heart, was suddenly swept away with my dreams, and I was to suffer for my failures, my broken promises to look after him, broken dreams and broken vows. I was realising just how evil I had been to make such promises, ones which I could never keep; I felt absolutely desperate.

Luke and Three had been through many such traumas, losing family, friends, colleagues, and so seemed to understand. They never asked what had changed my confidence. They just knew that the shock was realising itself and hitting me, but neither of them realised the truth, that I had killed him, left him to die in a desperate panic to save myself, and I couldn't tell them. I wanted to, but they would have hated me for it, after all, Luke never left Three to die, and they were all I had left in the world, with Mum and Cordelia locked away for their sins of destitution, so I went through the next few weeks trying hard to hide my grief by keeping busy, running around in the pub, going across the ferry to check for letters from Joshua, and forcing myself to look at the bridge. I never forgot the words from Luke, about looking and accepting, and he was right. Despite more nightmares about what I had done, I slowly managed to calm the despair. I know what Dad would have told me, 'life goes on, but so does the guilt'.

Several days had passed, the bridge had been removed and the boats again had free passage along the river. The talk in the pub was about the engineers and carpenters who were milling around, and on a couple of occasions, came into the pub for refreshment. It seemed that they were to make a temporary bridge across the river, where the old one had stood, since the new bridge which the rail company had permission to build was not yet built. At least Luke would get his customers back from the other side of the river.

I worked hard in the pub for my keep, not wanting to be a charity-case, and Mary helped me to learn the ways of the serving wench. I had a strange feeling that I was untouchable, as we worked our way around our designated tables, and Mary was continuously being groped, but nobody ever touched me. Don't get me wrong, it gave me a feeling of safety, but I had this nagging feeling of being 'untouchable', and I felt out of place, maybe a little curious, or maybe even a bit of jealousy. Why didn't they want me?

"Three, is there something wrong with me? Do I smell, or something?"

He laughed. "You smell beautifully, and yes, there is something wrong with you. Beauty can be a curse." He got on with his glass washing.

"That' stupid. They can't all be scared of my beauty. I'm not even that beautiful, so what's wrong with me?"

He moved over to a chair, sat down, and tapped the chair beside him. I sat with him.

"Now, Eunice, you must understand that these are simple fishermen. Most of them are married, but the ones who aren't probably *are* scared of you. These youngsters wouldn't know what to do with you, and besides, they're not good enough for a hero's daughter. They'd just drown and leave you in your hovel to struggle with the children. No good for you."

"But that shouldn't stop them trying. Don't they want to feel my.... you know what I mean." I hung my head.

"Now, listen carefully." He put his arm around my shoulders, and his Asian face frowned as he thought about his words. "They all want to feel your... you know what, but they're scared. The youngsters are scared of your beauty, they think they would just be rejected, and look like a cunt in front of their friends. So, they leave you alone. And the older ones, perhaps because they're married."

"That's not good enough! They all grab at Mary. They all want to feel her bits, and she's pretty. So, why not me?"

"Now stop that. You mustn't put yourself down, because you're a hero's daughter, a beautiful one, and they have good reasons not to touch you. They're scared of touching you, because they *are* scared!" He hesitated. "Haven't you noticed that they only touch Mary's breasts? They don't normally try to touch anything else, and if they do, she whacks them. Now, they know to stop at that point, because if they don't, they're out the door. No questions asked, straight out, headfirst. Now, you, if they even touch your tits, they're straight out the door, headfirst. They all know it. They've been warned." He looked me in the eye. "They all know who you are, and wouldn't want Peter Fuller coming up here to pound them into the ground."

It almost made sense, but, "Don't they know that my dad is dead?"

"No." He waved his head in thought. "We did wonder why you were in Yarmouth, but no, nobody knows. Except me, and I'm sorry to hear it. Please accept my condolences. But keep it quiet, the threat of him coming after them'll stop them trying to grab your fanny." He shrugged his shoulders. "I *am* sorry to hear, though."

He was sorry, I could tell in his face.

I sadly explained, "He died last autumn, influenza. Everybody cheered when it happened. Everybody hated him down there, and now I'm here, everybody loves him. Funny, but I don't think anybody knew who he was, even me. He never told me about the fight with Romany Joe, never told anybody. He was never a hero in Blythburgh, just a hated Estate Manager. And a detestable lay-preacher. Joshua said he was just living a lie, in hiding, to protect his family. I'm beginning to understand."

"Then let's let his detestable reputation stay in Blythburgh. It helps to be a hero up here, and a hero's daughter, so keep it to yourself, and I think Boss already knows, so you can talk to him about it if you need to. But don't mention it to anybody else."

As I thought about it, some sense filtered in, past the grey holes in my past memories, but it still kept nagging me.

"So, Three, please tell me the truth. If these people knew that Dad had died, what of it? Would I be at risk? What about the Gypsies? Wouldn't they come looking for me, like they did for Dad all those years ago? Wouldn't they want revenge for Joe Taylor's death?"

"Sorry, Eunice, but I don't know everything. This lot here would still be the same, scared to touch you, because of the hero that's looking out for you, Luke, but the Gypsies? Don't know about them. Perhaps you should ask Boss."

"Please Three, don't keep leaving loose ends. Why wouldn't this change towards me if they knew?"

"Because your dad wasn't the only hero around here. With one hero gone, there's another one stepped into his shoes, to look after you. Boss. He's a living hero, and they all know that, so you're safe. He never says much about Canton, but he was a war hero and should have got more than just the China War Medal, and will be remembered for his valour on a certain day on the streets, at least until I'm dead. Even then, I'll never forget it, it's the reason I'm still here to talk about it, and it's why they all respect Boss so much, because he's done it all before, and is scared of nobody, and when he had to, he proved it. And, it's not just about Canton. There was this young mush who was playing up about a year ago, and I was in the back when it started, so Boss sorted it. He took the man to the door and just threw him straight out, as if he was a rag doll. Boss knows how to contain any man, even though this one was a known fighter, but he was like putty in Boss's hands. Anyway, when he crashed to the ground outside, the fighter broke his leg, the long bone, and died about a week later. Nobody blamed Boss for the death, it was an accident caused by the man's bad behaviour towards others, but Boss did blame himself. He should have let me do it. But it did leave a reminder to the community what Boss was when he was in the navy, a specialist in war and killing, but Boss was quite upset about it. He never wanted to hurt the man, just get him out of the pub. Nobody talks about it, and that's how it needs to stay, in the past. But he's laid the rules down about you, and they all respect his rules. That's why they don't grope you. Scared of the consequences." He grinned. "Scared of me and Boss. I was his rear-guard in Canton. I still am, a real team." After a grinning session, "And there are other reasons why they don't grope you. But I can't tell you what they are, Boss'll be mad at me."

He seemed to be in a thinking session for some time, but then, "I wish I could tell you, but I think it'd be against the rules."

Peter Fuller's Daughter

CHAPTER 18
NOT GUILTY

It was an eye-opener on my known world. We were in the modern era, eighteen forty-five, when Britain civilises the World with its colonialisation and Christianity, and it was all so much more violent than I had ever imagined. It seemed that I had lived in a protected cocoon, closed off from the worst of the in-humanity and protected by a violent fighter, himself in hiding from his murderous sins. Now? I've moved bases, from one violent fighter to another. Some might say that I'm fortunate to have protection, but I'm not too sure, and only time will tell.

I continued to get out into the bar, serving the men and the occasional lady, and they all respected Luke's rules. They left me alone, most of the time. One young man, who had just come back from a fishing stint, grabbed my ass, so, I smacked him around the head, as Mary would, and he left me alone. I gave the lad a look which I believe he understood, a silent 'leave well alone or face the two Opium War heroes'. He never attempted to touch me again. Those drinking men were hardworking fishermen, frustrated by their isolated working environments and the lack of mermaids in our cold waters, but they all showed genuine respect for me, for each other, for Mary and for the management, making me realise that the slums of Yarmouth were inhabited by human beings, not low-living animals as some would make me believe.

I had certainly lived a sheltered life, but was now learning that these people were no different to any other group of humans, they were a team, a culture, and some might say a tribe, like wolves; all for one and one for all, and fuck the rest. I slowly began to feel a part of it.

However, the nightmares continued.

On the fourth occasion of my macabre awakening, the two boys rushed into my room, but this time without their weapons of war. It was becoming the norm.

Luke, as usual, sat on the edge of my bed until I calmed down.

"Do you want to talk about it? It might help."

How could I? He would hate me for what I did, I left my brother to die in order for me to live, so I just whimpered, and went back to sleep.

A couple of days later, Three sat with me as Mary scrubbed tables. "You need to talk. You've got demons in your head, and they need to be flushed out, laid to rest. You can't mourn for the rest of eternity, it'll destroy you, so get the demons out here, with us. Me and Boss can fight them with you. And Mary. Your family."

It made a lot of sense, and I suddenly realised that being hated for what I did wouldn't be such a bad thing; I deserved it.

"All right. But please don't tell everybody else, even if you do hate me for it. Promise?"

He made a solemn promise on One's life, his dad's, and asked Mary to give us some space.

"I remember what happened. I remember it all. The crack, the people pushing us onto the rail, and then hitting the water, and then.... We sank, everybody was kicking out, and I held Brenda and James's hands so tightly, and I got water into my lungs and panicked." I needed to be quiet for several minutes, to think. Three was very patient, never once pushing me, so, after some very big breaths, "I panicked. I let go of their hands." I was beginning to cry, deep inside, and my breath kept arresting, but I managed to say it, and made my plea. "I killed him. Killed poor James, just to keep alive myself. I killed my own brother. And I killed Brenda." I was instantly calm, although guilty, and my breathing came back to a regular pant. "I let go of his hand. I let him die, just to save myself. I let go of his hand, and he was gone."

I burst into tears, and Three offered me his shoulder.

He said nothing while I got it out of my system, and when

he did finally look me in the eye, I was expecting the worst.

He bluntly said, "You never killed him, nor Brenda."

But I did, I knew it, and simply having him say that I didn't, wasn't going to make it all good. I pushed away from him so that I could see his face.

"I killed him! And you can say what you want, but it won't change anything."

"I know, but if I can explain, it just might. You see, Eunice, many millions of people have blamed themselves for death, but, unless you kill somebody, then it probably isn't your fault. You lost James and Brenda in the river, you never killed them. Letting go of their hands? That's not murder. And, your dreams are probably wrong, confused."

"But, what if I could have saved him, and even Brenda? What then? I might have done."

"Never! You couldn't even save yourself, let alone James. When Boss grabbed you, you were gone, and whatever you did, it would never have saved James."

"You don't know that! What do you know?" I was beginning to get angry. "You don't know, you're not God!"

"But I am, I am God, and you don't know that I'm not, do you? I could be God, don't know which one, but if I am one of the Gods, I would never let you take the blame for what *I've* done to James, because even Gods have their good side, and telling the truth is one of them. Truth? You let go because you had to, and if you hadn't, you'd have killed him. That's the truth. You had to let him go, or go with him, no choice, and had no time to think about it. You did the right thing and James'll tell you so, when you next see him, I promise."

He had an asiatic way of saying these things, which are just matter of fact, without any flowering nor exaggeration, nor without any proper sense of reality, and somehow he was soothing me. "But you said that if I hadn't let go I would have killed him? That don't make sense." I think his grasp of the English language was good, but not perfect.

He grinned, but never put the statement right. "You know, Eunice, one of the important rules of naval warfare is 'if you can't save the others, save yourself.' At least there'd be somebody to inform the relatives. And there'd be someone to fight another day, and that's you, fighting another day, another life, in another World, for James, and you need to live James's life for him, not waste his life wondering what could have been. Life and death both go on, James will tell you that when you see him. So, you had a choice, save yourself, or save him. You made a hero's choice, and one day you'll understand, as you would never have saved both of you, so, think about it. But, however you think about it, you're not guilty of anything bad. Never. You made the right choice. I promise."

He stood up abruptly, nodded to Mary, then went into the back room.

CHAPTER 19
A MILLION MILES AWAY

I always knew that I could never have saved James, only hold his hand all the way to Heaven. Three's little piece of knowledge had begun to rattle around my head, and I was starting to think that I came out from the water for a reason. Was it to marry Luke, who saved me, or was it to save Mum and Cordelia from the workhouse?

I continued to take a daily trip across the ferry, as Luke had paid a travel subscription for the four of us, then walk into town to check my mail. I did it every day, mostly alone, but on two occasions Luke walked with me. He was well known, and, I think, well respected, but I never could tell if it was through the fear of what would happen if they never respected him, or through friendliness. I was erring on the side of friendliness, but again, only time will tell. He had a fearsome reputation, and a mystical, Asian right-hand man to boost that reputation, but was also kind and loyal. He had a lot of good bits, and I think Cordelia would approve of this suitor.

I was thinking a lot less about James, and more about Cordelia and Mum, with Three's naval wisdom beginning to make sense. James was gone, and Mum and Cordelia were here, and so was I. That was the fact of life, as I knew it.

On one of my trips into town, I first watched the workmen who were starting on the building of the temporary bridge. They worked hard to raise the chains between the towers, which would hold the wooden span, and one of them told me that it would all be done in a few weeks. Luke would get some of his customers back. It was important, as I didn't want my possible suitor to go bust, even before he marries me; Luke was slowly becoming part of my escape plan.

Anyway, I caught the ferry onto the Yarmouth side and

wandered off towards town, and the police station. The usual residents were scrubbing clothes and emptying sewerage, but, as I went past the Union Arms, I bumped into a familiar face. It was the boy from the whisky maker's.

"Wotcha. Where you going?"

I explained what I was doing, then he said, "Old Lanky's gone! The church picked him up when he smashed the house up." He looked around to ensure privacy. "They say he's been taken to another church, but the other day we delivered to the looney bin, and guess who was there, old Lanky."

"Working?"

"No, he's one of the loonies. Locked up with the rest of the weirdoes, they say, never to come out. Lost it!"

For some reason it saddened me, but he could have been a danger to weaker people, so it was probably justice.

"And, more to tell." He again checked that the coast was clear. "Someone's been asking after you. A mush who lives down the road, towards Lowestoft. He says he owes you. Don't know why he can't come looking for you himself, but he asked me to look out for you. He's in a caravan behind Rose Cottage, and he's a gypsy. Be careful if you go there, and take the landlord. He'll look after you."

I thanked the boy, and moved on towards the police station, then it occurred to me that, if the church has got old Lanky out, they will have put a new vicar in. It could be Joshua. So, I quickened my step and hurried out towards The Vicarage, past the police station, and was soon at the front drive. The grass had been neglected, and I almost convinced myself that Joshua had moved in, and I would proudly scythe the lawn for him. After staring at the front door for ages, I moved to it and pulled the bell chain.

The door opened.

"Yes?"

It was a man of about thirty, short and dumpy, with a collar, and very disappointing.

"Good morning, Sir. Do you know Joshua Reed?"

He nodded and replied, "Yes, a little. The Ipswich man. Why do you need him?"

"I'm a good friend, and I've been trying to contact him, but no response. I wondered if he might have come here, as the new vicar."

"Well, if things hadn't happened as they did, he may have done, but before Mr Ashcroft was retired, Mr Reed was given a new parish in Dorset. It was a good move for him."

Dorset, never heard of it. "Is it far from here, Sir?"

"Not sure how far, but must be at least two hundred miles."

Might as well be the gold mines in Bolivia, I could never find him. My mood dropped, and I wondered why he hadn't told me himself, but I suppose he could have already been gone by the time my letter reached him. I had never sent a letter before, and knew little about the new postal system, and how reliable it might be.

As I mooched back towards home, I decided that I should still check the police station, just in case, and blow me down, they had a letter for me! In my excitement I almost wet myself, but held on, all the way back to the Vauxhall Room, and sat down in front of the fireplace. Strange, but I had this feeling that I might want to burn the letter, but the bloody fire hadn't yet been lit, so I leaned back and just looked at the crumpled envelope on the table in front of me.

"Well, open it! It won't open itself." Mary urged me on. "Read it out loud."

Last time I read it out loud it was bad news for Cordelia's family. I didn't really want to.

"I'll read it quietly, first, just in case." I opened the envelope, and took out the single piece of writing paper. It was from Joshua, as I had expected, and was beautifully written in ink, just like my dad's handwriting. But the important thing was the message, not the package. It said very little, except that he hoped we were all fine and that Mr Ashcroft was behaving himself, and that he had moved parishes, to Dorchester in Devon. He at least gave me his address. I noticed that it was written before the bridge collapse, and probably before he ever received my letter, if he ever has received it. It was disappointing, but not the end of the World, since I could now write to him, and maintain a contact. Whether I would ever see him again, was doubtful. I read it to Mary.

"Never mind, at least you can tell him what's happened." She smiled. "Do you have any good news to tell him?"

"What do you mean? What about?"

She nudged up to me and whispered in my ear. "Boss. What about Boss?"

"What about him? He's a kind friend, that's all, and I'm only fourteen, that's if it's weddings you're suggesting."

"You look older than fourteen, and besides, nobody knows when your birthday is, so it's when you tell them. You can be sixteen whenever you want, especially here."

I didn't know if I had given clues, or if Luke had been talking, so I needed to ask him. But that was for another day, as I was keen to write a letter back to Joshua, with all the gory details, and probably no good news. I had one stamp left in my purse, so, I had to make it count.

CHAPTER 20
THE KROOLI

Unlike Joshua's letter to me, my letter was quite long; I had a lot to tell him, and I tried to tell him everything, at the same time reminding myself of everything. Writing it down was very good therapy, and helped to clear my head of some of the confusion which rattled around in it. By the time I had finished, I knew a lot more about what had happened over the previous few weeks. Funny how advice sinks in, then comes to the fore at a later date, like Lukes advice to look hard at the situation and you'll get used to it and move on. I was feeling stronger, alive, looking forward, and suddenly I wanted to succeed, no idea what at, but I knew that I would think of something.

One thing that I decided to do, was to sort out Luke.

"I keep hearing that you want to marry me. Is that true, or just rumour?"

He was set back by the question, and went bright red, then, "Where did you hear that? Who said it, and I'll put them right."

"You saying you didn't say it, or have you just changed your mind? You need to tell me, else I'll have to marry somebody else. Plenty of suitors come in here, some with their own boats, and are men of substance." I felt rather brattish, but good.

Eventually he did it, and was very brave. "I did mention it when we were having a drink in the bar one night. You were in bed. Shouldn't have said anything, and I'm sorry."

I was getting confused. He was like a little school-boy, scared of his own feelings, despite being scared of nothing else. But I wasn't scared of my feelings, we talked about all sorts at home, and honesty was important, so I was going to say what I thought! I suddenly remembered what Joshua had told me, 'keep your opinionated mouth shut until you're sure'. But I ignored it. "Why don't you just say what you bloody mean. Do you want to marry me, or not? Then we can get on with our lives, one way or the other. Well?"

He relaxed, smiled and very gently said, "Thanks. You've made it a lot easier, and you know that I want to."

"So, when're you going to ask me? Just wanting to won't get you what you want, and I ain't enlisting in your navy, we're talking about a life-long partnership, marriage, you have to grab it, if you want it. So, ask me, or shut up about it, especially with the others!"

After shaking his smiling head a few times, "You're so strong, so, I'll do as I'm told. Will you marry me?" He held his hand forward and held mine. "Eunice Fuller, will you be my wife?"

What? He had actually asked me, and all the crap that I'd just put him through, was turning on me. I didn't know what to say. I didn't know if I even *wanted* to marry him, I just wanted to know if he wanted to marry me. I suddenly felt very evil.

'Keep your opinionated mouth shut until you're sure'. I should have followed Joshua's advice, and waited until I had my own answer before worrying about Lukes's answer, but I had no idea if I wanted him in that way.

"I'm sorry, Luke. I don't know. I'm not even old enough, so, I don't know what to say. That's not 'no', it's 'I don't know yet'."

He endeared himself to me even more by accepting it as a 'maybe'. I would let him know very soon, is how we left it, but I did stress that I couldn't marry him until I was sixteen, even if the answer was to be 'yes'. He understood.

Before we went about our duties, he stated, "I'm so pleased with your answer. I was convinced it would be 'no'. Now, I can carry on living in hope."

My life was way too complicated, for a simple farm-girl.

Anyway, the other thing bandying around in my head was

the man who was looking for me, out towards Lowestoft, the one the whisky-boy told me about. I decided to take a chance to check it out. I probably should have told Luke about it, and asked him to accompany me, but I had this feeling that it was personal family business which may need to be kept in the family. I took a chance on it.

On my way, I stopped at the whisky maker's to check with the boy about the stranger's address.

"It's down towards Lowestoft, you'll see the looney bin over to the left, then a bit up on the right. Rose Cottage. The man who's asking about you, lives in a gypsy caravan in the back. About a twenty minute walk, that's all."

The road was muddy in places, and I found myself getting dirty shoes and mud-stained socks, and was worried about what the man would think of me, so, I walked along the short lane to the Asylum to see if they had somewhere that I could clean up. The staff were kind and let me sit in the office to clean my feet. There was a dark feeling about the whole place, and when some wailing began from the main building, it frightened me. I thanked the staff and got on with the short journey to the gypsy caravan. All the time I kept telling myself that this was an asylum, not a workhouse. The workhouse would be different, surely.

When I arrived at Rose Cottage, I looked towards the back of the property, where a gypsy caravan was parked. The grass around the wheels had grown up, so it was static, but it had been well maintained and looked to be lived in. The whisky boy said that the man lived in a caravan, I guessed that this was it. The tiny thatched cottage was, on the other hand, not well maintained, the thatch being old and rough and the windows dirty, so I never banged on the front door, assuming the house was unoccupied. I wandered down the side of the cottage.

"What d'you want?" The voice came from the front door which opened. "Who you looking for?"

I walked back to the front and there stood an old man,

who looked like he looked after himself about as well as he looked after his home. He wore loose breeches and a smock, with a head-scarf.

"Sorry Sir, I'm told that a man who lives in the caravan wishes to talk to me."

"And you are?"

"I'm Eunice." I suddenly felt nervous. "Eunice Ashcroft, Sir."

"Well, you'd better come in, then."

He stood aside for me to pass, and I found myself standing in a very dark room, with a small dining table and two chairs, and nothing else. The two windows were dirty, allowing very little light through.

"Take a seat, Eunice. I've been wanting to meet you for over ten years. Been a long time."

We sat at the table, opposite each other, and he just stared at me.

"Please don't be afraid of my stare, it's because I can't see very much. My eyes have almost gone. Anyway, tell me about yourself, for example, why you called yourself Ashcroft. You know he's in the asylum, down the road?"

"Yes, I've heard. He took the death of Mrs Ashcroft very poorly."

"And the whisky and laudanum. All finally caught up with him. Should've stayed out in Lanky, didn't like the man." He continued to look at me, but I wasn't sure how much he could see. "You're very pretty, I think. Are you?"

I smiled at his failing eyes. "My best friend, Cordelia, thinks so. She says I should marry a rich man, and she could be my lady-in-waiting."

"Is she pretty?"

"No, not very. Got a giant conk, and she says her face is like a cunt."

"Some cows have pretty asses!"

"That's what I told her! It's in the eye of the mush."

"You mean the beholder. The eye of the beholder. It's

strange how everybody has become prettier, since my eyes started to go. She should get out with a blind man, she'd be beautiful to him."

We prattled on for a bit, then I had to ask him. "Why do you wish to see me, Sir?"

"Well, I'm Romany, not a sir, so it's Sampson to my friends. Sampson Heron at your service, Lady Fuller. And, I've been wanting to meet you for many years. In the early days, I wanted to meet your father, and I sent my nephews down to look for him, without any result. I even went myself on one occasion. We found Joshua Reed, but he denied any knowledge of where your dad was, and then the Sherrif got involved. I had to just wait, and now my wait is over. You're here."

I was beginning to worry about my safety, so looked towards the door, which was not locked. I wasn't a prisoner, so I asked, again, "Why do you wish to see me, Sampson Heron?"

"In the early days we wanted to see your dad. You probably weren't even born, so it was all about the champion. He was a big name in our circles, the biggest name, and we had lost our old champion. Did you know that our man, Romany Joe Taylor, died after the fight with your dad, and Joe was a renowned fighter, probably the best ever. That was, until he met your dad. He was going to fight Joshua Reed, but Reed pulled out with a damaged wrist, even before the fight had started, so your dad stood in as his champion. Nobody knew of Peter Fuller, so all the money went onto Romany, and it was so much that I would have been killed if he had won, because I got my numbers wrong. I could never have paid out the bets if he'd won, and nobody would take any lay-offs, so, they would have slaughtered me, and even if they didn't kill me, they would have bankrupted me. Did I mention that I was the krooli, the man taking the bets? But Romany never won, Peter Fuller won. There were only a couple of bets on Fuller, they were the man you know in the

Vauxhall, and Lord Maybush. I had a moneybag which was bulging, and it was all on the loser, so most of it was mine. I made a fortune out of it." He stopped for thought, but I was an impatient teenager and leaned over to push his arm, to get on with it.

"Oh yeah, why do I wish to speak to you? I suppose you already know about the fight, so, moving on.... Romany Joe was dead. The entire fighting community was in mourning, not because he was a nice person, but because they all needed a fighter to use, so, they tried to find your dad, to make him an offer. A serious offer. A contract. Nobody ever found him, probably for the best for him."

"Were they going to hurt him?"

"Sort of. They wanted to take him on as their champion, to fight their corner, as Romany Joe did, so if they'd found him, and he agreed, he probably would've died in the ring, eventually, as Romany Joe did. Fighters always lose, in the end. Glad nobody found him, else you wouldn't be here." He smiled. "Now, I was looking for him for a different reason. In the ruckus that followed Romany Joe's collapse, Reed and your dad legged it back to Suffolk in fear of the crowd, probably sensibly at the time, but they never picked up the purse. That's why I need to speak to you, not just because you're Romany royalty, but because I've looked after the purse for your dad ever since." He stood up, slowly went out to the back room, and returned with a small, canvas bag. "This is your inheritance. The purse that belongs to your dad." He handed me the bag.

I gingerly looked inside, and there were gold sovereigns. "This mine? Really?"

"Really. It was tempting at times, but I've never needed any money since the fight. I made my fortune from the bets, so, this is your dad's reward for the win. There's a hundred sovereigns. All yours."

I almost fainted. I'd never even touched a sovereign, let alone owned a hundred. I couldn't believe it.

"Why? You could have spent it, done what you wanted with it, but you kept it all these years. Why?"

"Because I'm a Romany, and we have our pride and our standards, and we respect our royals, Your Ladyship."

'Now he's taking the piss.'

"And besides, I've never needed it. I made my money on the fight, so didn't need to upset our legends by stealing what was theirs. But, all joking aside, your dad's name has gone down in Romany history, so we have our traditions of loyalty towards our special heroes and heroines, and Romany tradition is strong, believe you me. You are in the one place in the World where nobody would dare to touch a hair on your head. Your dad will be admired for many years, and you are part of him." He bowed his head, then, "At your service Your Ladyship." He burst out laughing.

Peter Fuller's Daughter

CHAPTER 21
MADAME MARY

Mr Sampson gave me a mug of beer from his back room.

"It's only weak, but it won't give you the shits. There's a lot of it in the town at the moment. Always boil your water, or drink beer." We toasted our new friendship, then drank. "And, keep quiet about the money. Nobody knows you've got it, so nobody will try to take it. I told everybody that I gave the purse to old Maybush to pass on, years ago, but if I had actually given it to Maybush, your dad would never have got it. Not a nice man, Lord Maybush, with few morals. But, he did tell my relatives that he hadn't seen your dad since the fight, so, not all bad. The whisky boy told me that you lived on the Maybush estate. Your brother told him, when they played outside Lanky's house." He huffed. "A good source of gossip, that whisky boy, but don't ever tell him anything, unless you *want* the World to know." He touched his nose.

Mr Heron kindly walked me home, as far as the river. He said that it would help to cement my standing as a Ladyship, being seen with the krooli, and it would guarantee my safety. He told me again that I was Romany Royalty, and they were loyal towards their special ones. I must admit, I had only ever heard bad about the gypsies, but perhaps all gypsies weren't all Roma, all having different morals.

When I got back home, Luke and Three were keen to know about my visit, as the whisky boy had made a delivery, and, of course, gossiped. It confirmed what Mr Heron had said about the compulsive talker; don't tell him anything.

"It was really interesting. It was the man from the fight, who you told me about, who took the bets, and he wanted to meet me, and tell me how being the daughter of a Romany bare-knuckle legend, made me Romany Royalty." I scoffed, and Three laughed, then stood up and bowed. "And he said that I would be safe in Yarmouth, as the gypsies would look out for me."

Luke grinned. "Romany Royalty? That doesn't mean they won't steal from you, given half the chance."

"Mr Heron said that it won't happen. They all respect their special ones and their families, even if we are gadjes, so don't knock it!"

"Wasn't knocking it. But whatever, it's better than being their enemy. So long as they respect you, you'll be all right with them. But don't expect them to fight for you."

"Why not?" I was feeling relaxed, and playful. "They'd put their lives on the line for their Princess Eunice. My family are worshiped, so there." I blew him a raspberry. "And don't tell me they're any different to you, since you put your life on the line for your Queen, down in Canton. No different!"

Three was seeing the funny side, but instantly went serious. "And Boss, you'd put your life on the line for your Princess Eunice. Wouldn't you?"

It was nice to talk crap, it kept my mind well away from the sovereigns. I needed some quiet time, alone, to consider those, and Mr Heron's mention of 'nobody knows, so nobody will try to take them', was good advice, and they stayed safely stashed in my room. I found a loose floorboard to put them under. It wasn't that I never trusted Luke and Three, it was more that I didn't really know. I would never get another nest-egg like it, for the rest of my life, so it needed protecting, and it wasn't just about a hundred sovereigns, it was about a new life for my family.

The next day seemed a lifetime away from my visit to Mr Heron's, as I scrubbed tables with Mary. She never talked much, but when she did, I always found it to be worth listening to.

"That old man that you visited, he used to be head of their band, and was the top man on the kris. That's like a gypsy court, and decides all their issues, for the whole tribe, like our courts do. He's a well-known man. I think he was their vovid.

Not really sure what that means."

"But he's not living with the tribe. Was he chucked out?"

"Well, if you go further past his house, his family often camp on a field which is owned by your old friend. I don't know why he lives separately from them."

One of my dad's jobs was to make sure the caravans never got parked on the Maybush Estate. He always hated that part of his work, and showed some respect for the travellers, and always said to call them Roma, not gypsies. I think gypsy is a derogatory term, as is pikie.

"He's not a gypsy, he's a Roma. That's what my dad would have said, if he was here. He said it was a pejorative word, meaning insult or belittling. Shouldn't really say the word."

"All these clever words!" She thought for a bit. "Have you ever had you palm read?"

"Nah, it's against the law, ain't it?"

"Probably, but you know what laws are, for the poor, and you know what the law's like, too many other things to worry about, so it's only illegal if you're poor and get caught." She looked around, to make sure we were alone. "Can you keep a secret, a real one?" She accepted my nod. "Well, my mum's family were gypsies, or Roma, and settled down near here. Became normal. Anyway, she's taught me about palm reading, and I think I'm good at it." She again looked around. "Don't ever tell anyone, please."

I expected her to carry on, but never, so I asked, "Well? Are you gonna do my palm?"

"Thought you'd never ask. But, since you've asked, I don't think it's illegal. I never tried to make you do it, so it's just between friends, not business. That's my story, Your Honour." She had a giggle to herself, then reached over to take my hand and held it palm-up. "Ah yes, I can see a long lifeline, many years into the future, but you've recently lost loved ones. I can see, though, that you will soon get some new loved ones, but still search for your old ones, and then you'll marry a tall, fat stranger, and he'll look after you for the rest of his life. You'll outlive him, as he'll get fatter and die early, leaving you with your fortune." She felt around my hand a bit more. "Yes, I can see it, but it's very blurry, and a little boy is telling you to get up, and get on, and to stop blaming yourself. Can't see what for." She gently laid my hand on the table.

I didn't know quite what to say, so I told the truth. "That was very clever rubbish. And Luke isn't that fat."

"Is, and he's getting fatter every month! You've been here more than a month, haven't you noticed? And besides, who said I was talking about Luke? Well, was I? Hey, is it Luke?" She grinned, then looked around, again. "That mean you're marrying Luke?"

"No! I'm not sixteen for nearly two years! So, no, not at the moment." I felt under a little bit of pressure. "I spoke to him, and he wants me to, but I'm not old enough. Leave it at that."

"I've hit a nerve, I can see that."

"You have, so leave it. And I don't want you talking about it to anyone else, right? You'll just have to wait and see!" I took a deep beath, then, "Sorry, but I've been worrying about it. Anyway, that was all very clever how you made all that up. Is that how the gypsies do it? Get a bit of knowledge, then make the rest up? And who am I gonna keep searching for?"

"Your mum and Cordelia, of course! Who else?"

I felt such a strange jolt as soon as she said it. She couldn't possibly know about them, unless somebody else had told her, namely Luke. I was suddenly wondering if I really wanted to marry an old woman of a gossip, and a fat one at that who was getting fatter and would die early, according to Madame Mary, and my life again clouded in my head. But, perhaps Mary was the one who could help me through my quandary, just two years older, but probably much wiser.

"Do you think I could get them back? Do you even know where they are?"

"Yeah, the whisky-boy said that they're in a workhouse. Your brother told him. And, why couldn't you? All you have to do is marry Luke, and they've got somewhere to live and work. That'd get them out the workhouse. Simple. All you need to do is make sure he agrees, before you say yes."

'Well, she's a dark horse.' Not just a plain face, but an accomplished conniver.

Peter Fuller's Daughter

CHAPTER 22
HERE'S TO US

Life was not getting any simpler, but when I thought about it, it was getting clearer. All I had to do was to stop the nightmares, protect my inheritance which Dad fought for, juggle my emotions between Luke and anybody else who may wish to marry me, and to do my bit of work every day in the pub for my keep. I'm sure many, many other young girls were having a much harder life in eighteen forty-five, but it's a strange human phenomenon in that we never think like that, and no matter how bad somebody else's hell is, yours is the only one that matters. I'm not sure if it's plain selfishness, or the will to survive.

Anyway, Mary's words kept coming back to me. All I had to do was to do a deal with Luke, and I would be able to get Mum and Cordelia out, after all, they were suffering much more than me. My mind was made up.

"Mary." She came over and sat opposite me. "Yesterday you said that a little boy was telling me to stop blaming myself. What did you mean?"

She shook her head. "Don't know. It just came to me."

"But you just made it all up, like all the palm readers."

"Yes, but...." She stood up to return to her cleaning, but hesitated. "I saw a little boy in the sky, and he told you. That's all I remember."

What a load of twaddle. She was so convincing with her lies, that she had convinced herself, so, I decided to ignore it. It couldn't have been James, because he was lost in the river, I think.

Moving on, I had to make a deal with Luke. If I was to agree to marry him, he would have to let me take in Mum and Cordelia. Should I get it in writing? I knew that Luke could read and write very well, but making a written contract all seemed very un-loving, cold, and I never wanted a cold married life, but what were the options?

The sovereigns! Could I get Mum and Cordelia out of the workhouse, and live on that money. It was a lot of money, but not enough to get a property, certainly not in Yarmouth, and probably not enough in the country. Then we'd have to feed, by working, so, the country was not the right place, it would have to be a town with industry. We could go up north to the cotton mills, or to Norwich to the silk mills, but I'd rather live a cold married life than live in the hovels that the cotton workers have to share, and all die early from cholera or blisters. As much as I wanted to marry somebody I loved, Luke was looking the most realistic option. Don't get me wrong, I really liked him, admired his kindness, but his ruthless attitude towards violence and death frightened me. My dad was clearly a fighter, but he left that life behind, and the pub industry would never allow Luke to turn his back on it, and the pub was his life, so why should he turn his back on it? I had a lot of thinking to do over the next week, which was how long I gave myself to decide. My path forward was unclear.

A couple of days had passed, and the temporary wooden bridge was due to open. It was never a big ceremony, being opened by the chairman of the railway, George Stephenson, and the first thing they did was to dismantle the toll booth. It was to be free to cross for all. Vauxhall was again connected to Yarmouth, and the railway ruled. It was a sad period for the wherrymen, who had always been the main means of goods transport to Norwich, but the railway suddenly became the flavour of the year for the other locals. It would even save much of the road traffic past Acle, a route which was renowned for ambush and robbery. The docks could bring in more coal and steel, and the fishermen could send their fish nationwide, and the goods could come into Yarmouth from all over England for export across the sea. It was an exciting time for Britain, for some.

I watched the first people to cross. It was a single lane bridge, with a bridge-keeper each side to make sure that only one cart was on the bridge at any one time, and then a group of pedestrians were allowed over, but not allowed to stop. In view of what had happened quite recently, many of the pedestrians waited at the tower, to build up the courage, and then run as fast as they could to the other tower, not daring to look down nor loiter. But once a few carts had crossed, and a few groups of pedestrians, it was deemed safe by The Mayor, and many people celebrated. Luke was one of them.

Suddenly The Vauxhall Room was busy again. The circus had gone, and the rail users were using the bridge, instead of the ferry, and all coming past our front door. Many were coming in for their refreshments, and the business boomed.

Luke called us together one night, after the last of the drinkers had left, for a celebratory drink. With myself, Luke, Mary and Three around the table, each with a shot glass of special whiskey, from Ireland, the toast was raised. Luke raised it.

"Here's to Queen Victoria, and our future together, right here in The Vauxhall Room."

We raised our glasses, then downed the whiskey and banged the glasses on the table, like a four-gun salute, and thought about grimacing at the harsh taste, but it wasn't harsh like the local stuff, but smooth, superior, all the way from Ireland. We all smiled.

Mary held her head low as she grinned at me, and I knew what she was thinking; 'all here together, with Mum and Cordelia'. I was thinking the same, but said nothing.

That night I had another frightening dream, about James. It just went over and over with my hand slipping from his. I screamed. Luke rushed in, as he always did.

CHAPTER 23
PETER FULLER'S DAUGHTER

Mary thought that I had missed an opportunity to approach the subject, after the toast, but I still wasn't sure about it. I still had two days left before making my decision.

The pub had been busy after those first few days of the new bridge, with people coming over from the other side, and railway users dropping in as they passed, and I finally plucked up the courage to go across. I went to check for letters from Joshua, but there was nothing.

On my way back, I noticed that I was following a group of about ten men and women, all adorned with colourful Roma attire and jewellery, and one of them was my friend Sampson Heron. It looked like he was being escorted by the group, and they were moving very slowly, so I slowed myself, to make sure that I never caught them. It was the first time that I had ever looked carefully at a group of Roma, but, apart from their colourful traditional dress, they weren't very impressive. They were all skinny and quite short, probably undernourished and stunted.

The colourful group went directly to the bridge, and then stopped to wait for their permission to cross. After a cart had made the crossing into Yarmouth, they were waved on. They were all very wary, but Sampson ordered them across, and they hurried over and went straight on, towards the pub. The group stopped outside the pub, waiting for Sampson to give the order.

I suddenly felt afraid for Luke and Three.

I hurried over the bridge and caught them up, outside the pub, and loudly said hello to Mr Heron. I wanted Luke or Three to hear me.

"Well, here she is, our Queen! This is Miss Fuller, in case any of you haven't yet seen her beautiful face." He took my hand and kissed the back. "We've come to honour you." He smiled, as if he was about to say something big, but the door opened. It was Luke.

"Eunice. Is everything all right? Are these your friends?" He stepped over to me, and suddenly Three was at the door. Luke nodded to Mr Heron. "Good day Sampson. Are you meeting somebody here?"

The group were tense, and a couple of them played with their earrings.

"Good morning Luke. Yes, we've come to meet Eunice. To honour her."

Nothing else was said, as Luke went into the pub, followed by the entire group, and Three at the rear. There was a sharp tension coming from the group, which then spread to the other customers, who moved over to one side to give the group seating space. I went to the side, near the serving door.

I quickly studied the Roma, and they didn't look like hard men, undernourished but beautifully dressed, and the three women were wearing blue head-scarfs, and gold on their necks and faces. One had a striking gold wrist band which looked like it could be very valuable. Their ages were difficult to judge, but were all full adults, apart from one young man, probably about fourteen or fifteen.

Mary served them with their drinks, and Three assisted her. Luke gave me a facial message, ordering me not to serve. Like me, he was intrigued by the 'honour' which Sampson had mentioned. In addition to intrigue, I felt a touch of darkness in my heart, and, looking at the nervous faces of the other customers, I wasn't alone.

"This is a nice pub, Luke!" Mr Heron raised his glass to Luke, and nodded to Three. "Good job the bridge is back."

I never knew until later that the Roma in the Yarmouth area were wary of boats, and would never use the ferry. Mary told me that they would rather swim across a river, than float over it, nobody being able to tell the history behind it. The other customers were fishermen, probably much more respectful of the water, but not afraid of it.

About an hour had passed, with there being quite a few beers drunk, and brandies for the ladies, and lots of talk amongst themselves which I couldn't understand, and the occasional polite exchange between them and the fishermen, but not a lot else. Then Sampson stood up. The little old man looked at me.

"May I request the presence of our Queen, Lady Eunice Fuller?" He waved me over.

Luke grabbed my arm, and walked me to the table. He was clearly concerned about something.

"This is, as most of you will know by now, our Queen. We haven't had one for some years, and it's time to revive tradition, with the daughter of the greatest knuckle fighter ever known, to be part of our legends." He looked me straight in the eye. "Eunice, this is my youngest son, Kaven." He put his frail old hand on the youngest boy's shoulder, "You're going to marry him."

I almost fainted. Luke held tightly onto my arm, then sat me down on a seat by the fire. I was shocked.

"Sampson!" Luke stomped back to Mr Heron. "Take you traditions elsewhere. We're not pikies." He stood menacingly in front of Mr Heron, and the entire pub froze. Three hovered. "Eunice isn't for sale, nor up for grabs. We respect our women, so she'll marry who she wants. Get out!"

Mr Heron calmly smiled. "I heard a little rumour, that you wanted to marry her. Is that why you're stomping? Jealousy? If so, you know what it's about, a fight for the girl. You up for it?"

"This ain't about me, it's about Eunice. It'll be her choice, ask her!"

Luke carefully stood aside, so that Mr Heron could see me. I looked at the ground.

"Well Eunice, your Ladyship? Is it about you, or is it about Luke? My son is royalty, but what's this mush, a bar tender? Or is he more? Will he fight for you?"

The man that I briefly admired was nothing but a thug, with his boys waiting in the aisles, his lackies, and not one of them with their own minds, just pikie ass-lickers. I felt my dad coming out in me.

"It's about me! Just me, Peter Fuller's daughter!" I jumped forward. "Heron, get out of my pub! Now! I won't marry any of your family, ever, and if you think you can change that, you're an idiot. You think you're the King, well perhaps you are, but King of fuck-all. Take your pikie shit out of my life and don't come back!"

He just laughed. "Seen it all before. It's not up to you, it's up to me, and my family, so, go and sit down like a good little Lady, and let the men do the business." He stood up and faced Luke, who was about a foot taller, much younger, and upright. "My son's champion will fight you, Luke. If that's what you want."

Suddenly Three was there from nowhere. "I'm Boss's champion. Where's yours?"

The centre of the pub cleared, with the fishermen on one side and the Roma the other, with Luke, Three, Sampson and one of his boys in the middle. I moved to the serving door, with Mary.

"Don't let them do it, Mary. Please."

"Nobody's going to stop them. Just keep your head down and pray."

The four stood in front of each other, and Three asked, "What rules?"

Sampson Heron answered. "No rules, just an outcome. When one or other can't continue, they've lost, and if it's to the death, so be it."

Luke was shaking his head by this time, then he looked to me, apologising, but Three was up for it and stood in front of his opponent. The Romany was about the same size as Three with jet-black hair and a tint to his face. If his eyes were rounder, he could have passed as Three's relative. They shook hands.

The Romany first just stared Three out, who never moved. Three watched as his opponent drew a nine-inch knife from his trousers, but let him move around, threatening with the weapon, and looking for his opportunity. Three just waited. Then the Romany saw an opportunity to lunge with his knife towards Three's face, but the strike never landed. In one move, Three glanced the blade away, then swung around and stabbed his foot straight into the Romany's thigh. A loud, sickening crack, and Three stood over the pretender, who lay rigid on the floor, his right leg twitching.

Seconds, that was all it took, and Three had won me my freedom from the life a Romany. It sickened me, the whole episode, and I needed to sit in front of the fire in a heady swoon as the Roma left the building, carrying the loser. The last one to leave was Sampson Heron, who moved to stand in front of me.

"Well Eunice, you're still my Queen. I would have loved to have you in the family, but no hard feelings."

He left to join his family who waited outside.

Peter Fuller's Daughter

CHAPTER 24
THE DOWRY

It was over in not many minutes, the duel for my hand. It wasn't until after the Roma had gone that I began to feel physically sick about the whole thing, about me being put up as a prize in a fight. It wasn't even a personal fight. Luke's champion beat the Roma champion, and the two suitors never even got their hands dirty. I felt like a piece of meat on market day.

"Are you all right?" Mary sat with me by the fire, once the customers had gone. "No one expected that. You didn't know anything about it, did you?"

I shook my head. "Nothing." I was feeling very down on myself, not really knowing why, since I had done nothing wrong. "Why did it happen, Mary? I'm so confused."

She shrugged her shoulders, then looked towards the serving door, as Three came through it. "Perhaps he can explain."

Three sat down with us, looking very sheepish, considering he had just done the heroic thing. He went to say something, but held back.

Mary asked, "Why didn't you kill him? He'll probably be back for more, with his mates. You know you can't trust the gypsies, they think they're above the law."

Three shook his head and thought, before answering. "I think I did kill him. Didn't you hear the crack. His long bone's broke, and the gypsies ain't got no doctors. He'll die, most likely."

When I later thought about the fight, I could recall clearly how Three went for the long bone, deliberately and accurately, and with great power. He knew what he was doing, killing him without making a big spectacle of it, death from injuries, not murder.

Three assured Mary, "They won't take it further, believe me. They have their pride which is bruised, embarrassed, so will stay away, and besides, the krooli has a thing for Eunice, and he's their boss."

As he spoke, Boss came into the room, looking even more apologetic than Three had. He sat with us and looked at his lap. He was waiting for me.

"Why?" I looked into his face. "Did this have to happen? That poor boy.... gonna die."

"But...." He frowned. "Did you want to marry the pikie?"

What? I was set aback, with questions flying around like a whirlwind in my head. "No! I don't even know him! Why would I want to marry him?"

"Eunice, this's a harsh World, and we have to survive the harshness." Luke looked at Mary, before explaining. "If Three, or me, hadn't fought, you'd be marrying the pikie. It's not up to you, they arrange their marriages, and the bride has no say. Please believe me, I did it because I thought....." He stopped dead. After he again looked at Mary, he quietly apologised. "I did it so that you can make your own mind up. I know what you're thinking." He shook his head, then reached out and held my arm. "This doesn't mean you've got to marry me, just consider me, please."

He was almost too good to be true, and I was his dream. But, I mustn't let that cloud my judgement, although him being good is a big tick. But I'm not making my mind up, yet. Tomorrow.

I asked, "What if you'd not fought, and the gypsy was to marry me. I'd just say no."

Mary carefully answered. "As Luke has already said, it wouldn't be up to you. If you didn't go with them, they'd *take* you with them. They kidnap young brides, if she refuses. You've got to believe me, Eunice, the only way was to kill the challenger. That's their culture, lying, deceit, kidnapping, when it comes to marriage, and just in case they have another string to their deceit, stay indoors for a while." Mary had a surprising knowledge of Romany ways, she was descended from a gypsy family. "And now some of the tribes are wary of the law, and will buy the bride. However they do it, they'll give the dowry, then she belongs to them if it's accepted. They believe that the slave trade is still legal, so they think it's all right to buy ownership of a person, if the purchase price, the dowry, is accepted." She smiled like a holy man in his pulpit. "Never trust anything they tell you, they lie continually, if it suits them. My great nan was a gypsy slave."

The sovereigns! Does the krooli own me? He paid me well, or was he paying Dad, with a story of kindness, but were they all lies? Why was this happening? Does he believe he's paid for me with sovereigns, or was he being honest?

Three could see my face as I sweated, but never asked, just, "You know Eunice, where I come from is the Mã River, and our religion tells us that there are two Worlds living in one space, a good World and a bad World, and me and you live in the opposite World to the pikies. I believe we're in the good World, but that's just my opinion, so make sure you stay in this one. You wouldn't like theirs." After smiling at Mary, for some private reason, he suggested, "Stay with us, and you'll be fine. We're good people, and will live forever in our little bubble, right here."

Luke had a giggle. "Nicely put. You stick with us good people, and you'll remain good, and now you need to relieve yourself of any secrets you're harbouring. Secrets can fester into gangrene, then death, and then you'll be in the other World, and you wouldn't like that. Haven't your dreams told you that? So, what're you hiding in that pretty little head? There's something, and trust us, you wouldn't want gangrene, especially in the brain."

No, I can't tell! They just want my money, and they won't get it, it's for me, Mum and Cordelia, so I abruptly stood up and left for my room. The first thing I did was to check the money, under the loose floorboard, which was still there, and at the time it was all that mattered to me, my money. But then, was it a dowry, or a slave payment, or was it kindness? And which World is The Vauxhall Room really in, the good or the bad?

I lay on my bed and prayed.

CHAPTER 25
A FEW YEARS, YET

It took me a while to get to sleep, with my mind in a panic about ownership, ownership of me, that is, and it was becoming a living nightmare. I couldn't wait to get into a slumber, and away from this World, into my own from where I could wake when the going gets too torturous.

As always, my dreams were vivid. The old times on the Maybush Estate played a heavy role in most, and I vaguely remember Luke courting me, but he was in a white robe, with Three as his man-in-waiting, and Mary was in a long, vivid red dress and headscarf, like a Romany lady with my sovereigns hung around her neck. Every time I tried to grab the sovereigns, I couldn't quite reach, and as much as I moved towards her, she never got any closer, then my teeth began to fall out, leaving me spitting them over the floor, with Luke laughing. Then I roused, and the dream went. As soon as I was back in a sleep, I was in the river, desperately trying to hang onto James. It kept repeating, over and over again, as his hand slipped from mine but, for the first time, I felt I was sinking as my grasp broke from his, and the light from the surface becoming more and more distant. Then I woke up.

I never screamed, just lay wondering what had happened. I was falling away from him, downwards, and this had never been the case in my other dreams, he had always been falling away from me, so I tried to get back to sleep to return to my dream and seek an answer, but I couldn't sleep any longer. I lay on the bed for hours, until the daylight came, when I rose.

The first thing I did was to check under the loose floorboard. My sovereigns were still there. I promised myself that they would be protected with my life, and that Luke and Three would never get them, they were my inheritance. Or, were they my purchase price?

Whatever they were, they were mine to keep, and nobody would get them for as long as I was alive, not even Luke. I almost knew what was happening, but could do nothing to stop it. The money was taking over!

I was down early, and Mary turned up early, so we scrubbed the tables together, then sat in front of the unlit fire.

"You all right?" Mary frowned. "You look annoyed about something. Tell me."

I was just annoyed about everything. It was getting to me, and as I looked at Mary, all I could think of was my money, and that was what I think was annoying me the most, the money. I needed help.

"You know you did my palm, well, was it all made up?"

She grinned. "Most of it, but sometimes when I do it, I see things that I wasn't expecting. Not made up."

"So...." I hesitated, a little afraid of something. "So, will you do me again? See what comes up?"

She shook her head twice, then nodded and held her hand out for mine, which I offered, palm-up. She studied the lines, running her finger along the life-line, and spat into my palm. "You've got a long life-line, almost never-ending, but it keeps going, then coming back. And your thumb-pad is tight, as if it's waiting for something, or hiding something, stressed about something, maybe it's guilt. But you're not guilty, so it must be about greed. A secret is trying to take you under with it, to be buried and never revealed, going down deeper and deeper, never to return to this World, just floating around in the other World. You've...." She stopped, then let go of my hand and looked away. "Don't want to, any more." She stood up, stomped over to the serving hatch and began wiping down the shelf.

She left me wondering what she had seen, even if it was all made up.

"Mary, can I ask you a question? Please? Sit with me,

please?"

She slowly gave in, and came back to her chair. "I don't want to do it any more. It gives me a headache."

"All right, but can I ask you something personal, might even be stupid." I accepted her nod. "Well, why're you here?"

"Stupid! I work here, don't I. I get paid to be here, that's why."

"That's not what I meant. Why do you work here? Your family do the fishing, don't they? Why aren't you with your family? And besides, you said your mum and dad were dead."

After shaking her head a few times, she took a deep breath, and, "I am with my family. This *is* my family, and yours. This is *our* family, all we have, and no good thinking otherwise. This is our World, don't know if it's the good World or the bad World, don't know how you tell, but we're in it, just us and them." She jumped up and carried on with her cleaning work.

I was getting deeper and deeper into my World of confusion, which was rapidly merging with whichever World Mary was in, and I was being drawn to her like a magnet. She was so plain, un-educated, slap-stick with her manners, but oh, so attractive. It was today that I had to make up my mind about Luke and my future, but I felt that I was suddenly looking at my future, cleaning tables, and she wasn't so plain, after all. I was falling in love with Mary!

I never panicked, just asked her to come back to her seat. She did. I wanted her to tell me more about me, even if she was making it up.

"What do you really want from me?" She seemed defensive. "I can't tell you any more, so don't even ask."

"But why? Why can't you? Can't you tell me about James. I won't report you."

"Don't matter. I don't want you to know, and you don't want to know, and besides I tell the future, not the past. Past is gone." She smiled, perhaps nervously. "Nobody really wants to know their future, not all of it. And I can't just tell you what you want to know, it's not up to me, and what happens to you will happen whether I tell you or not, and there's no changing it, even if you know."

"But you just make it all up, don't you?"

"No! I don't make it all up. Not the important bits, and you don't want to know them, so *shut up* and don't ask again! I ain't telling you any more!"

She was getting annoyed, so I had a choice; walk away or change the subject. I changed the subject.

"Sorry. Didn't mean to upset you. Anyway, should I marry Luke?" Today was my day of decision. "I've got to make a decision today."

"Why? You've got forever to make your mind up. He ain't going anywhere, and nor are you!"

"What d'you mean, not going anywhere? I've got to go to Blything, get my mum and Cordelia out."

"Yeah, but it ain't gonna happen! It can't, just believe me, it can't happen, not here, not ever! Well, not yet, anyway."

Why can't it happen? I've got the sovereigns, I can get them out, even without Luke, I can.

Then Mary calmed down and quietly answered, "Yes, marry Luke. He's a good man, a bit fat, but loyal to the bone. Yes, marry him, but make him agree to take your Mum and Cordelia in, as staff. He might agree, but if he does, it'll be a few years yet before it can happen. Several years yet."

I was beginning to believe her. I had no idea what she meant, but I was sure that she was being honest. Perhaps she was casting some sort of spell over me, her old Romany blood in her young body. You know, witches used to be tortured and burned, but not any more, no, in eighteen forty-five they just have to pay their penalty by working in pubs, in Vauxhall.

"I'm gonna ask if he'll take them in, else I won't marry him. I'll tell him as soon as I see him, unless you tell me not to."

"Not up to me, is it! But, don't forget, it could be a few

years before it can happen. And, don't ask why."

I took her instruction, not to ask why. I'll have to ask Luke.

I asked, "Do you know anything about dreams? You know, nightmares?"

She grinned, as if to say 'why ask me?', but then nodded. "I do. I know that they're all in the head, not real. But my nan always said that they *are* real, until you wake up. Then they become a dream. What do you believe?"

"I used to think they were like fairytales, always end in happiness. But since James died, I've been plagued with bad dreams."

"Boss did say you were having some bad nights. Said you scream."

"I do. But not today. I woke up and wanted to get back to sleep, to my nightmare, because I couldn't understand any of it, but I couldn't sleep any more, so the meaning is lost. But, I think James is still alive."

She leaned over and took my hand. "Wherever he is, he's gone. You're here, and he ain't, so get on with your own future. He's gone. Or, to put it simpler, you've gone. Believe the dream, it's James talking to you, so stop feeling guilty, and live here, happily ever after. James can live his own life."

She sighed, then went back to her cleaning.

With the pressure of my sovereign induced greed, my nagging guilt, my grieving and confusion, I had to make my mind up.

"Mary, I've got to go back to Blythburgh."

She looked at me and calmly replied, "Oh well. We'll see." But, before I could get through the door, "Nice thing about this world is you can always change your mind."

Peter Fuller's Daughter

CHAPTER 26
OUT THERE

I was a little surprised by Mary's reaction. I expected her to advise me, tell me to marry Luke or to make a deal, to give it bit more thought, or even marry the Romany lad, but she simply said, 'Oh well. We'll see.' But, I can change my mind, apparently. So, I thanked her, for some reason, then went to my room to check my sovereigns. They were all there. Then, I looked out of the window to see what the weather was like, with a mind to just walk away, go south to Suffolk and get Mum and Cordelia out, then do whatever we could do to survive. The money would help us to set up a home and create some form of work.

The weather was fine, it was late June, perfect time of year for sleeping rough, so perhaps today was the day.

Then, as I looked to my right, towards the river, I saw them.

Joshua and James! It was them, holding hands and moving towards the river!

I ran downstairs, straight out of the front door and down to the river, then pushed past the people waiting to cross the bridge, but I never saw them. They were gone. I panicked, looking down the banks left and right, then across the bridge, and I had to get over there. There was a cart on the bridge, but it was almost across to the other side, so I ran over and squeezed past it, then pushed past the bridge keeper as he swore at me. But I still couldn't see them. Joshua and James were nowhere to be seen, simply gone. My panic waned and despair set in, and my breathing became frantic as I burst into tears. The people crossing the river just ignored me. I quickly pulled myself together, telling myself that it couldn't have been them, 'James is dead!'

So, with a heavy heart, I went back to the bridge tower,

where the bridge keeper was looking rather wildly at me. "What the hell you doing? You know the rules, you wait for my permission!"

He was a jobs-worth, but his bark was worse than his bite, especially when he saw my tear-drenched cheeks, so I asked, "Sir, have you seen a vicar and a little boy crossing?"

He frowned. "No vicars today. Why do you need him? Has he done something wrong?"

I shook my head as I looked along the river, both sides, but could see nothing. I had run out of the pub in less than a minute, so surely I would have caught them up, but where were they? Were they anywhere? I began to question my own sanity.

"Please Sir, if you see a vicar and a little boy, can you tell them to go to the Vauxhall Room. Please. I'm Eunice, the boy's sister."

He was a very limited man, who responded with pride when given some responsibility. "I know who you are, Miss and I'll look out for them. It'll be my honour to." He dopped his cap to me, which made me cringe.

So, I wandered back to the pub. Mary was waiting.

"Well? Catch it?" She smiled, but frowned at the same time. "Went after something, don't look like you got it."

I just lumped down in front of the fire, feeling a little numb. I never said anything.

Mary sat beside me, and put her arm around me shoulder. "Don't get down, there was nothing there, anyway. Never is."

"What do you mean, never is?" My numbness and despair was put to the back, momentarily, and my heckles began to stand up. "What the hell you on about? They were there, I saw them!"

She shook her head, like a mother, and gently told me, "No, they're never there. You just saw them, but they weren't there. Honest."

"How do you know? You don't even know what I saw!

146

How the hell can you say that?"

"Because it's true. We've all been there, and they've all gone, yours and mine, and Three's and Boss's. All gone, and they won't come back, ever."

I was getting more and more confused by the day, by the minute, and I was beginning to want to run away from this hell, The Vauxhall Room, from these three people who seemed all too good to be true, and probably were. I looked into Mary's face, studied it for a few second, and she was telling me something, with her dark eyes, they were piercing, even hypnotic.

"What're you trying to tell me? Please Mary, I don't know what's going on. It's starting to scare me."

"I know, but it's not all bad here, it's a good life, most of it, so mustn't be scared of it, and look outside at the rest, and ask yourself where you want to be. Ask yourself if you're better off or worse off than the others. Safe, warm, fed, loved. Go on, ask. Dare you."

"All right." I carefully thought about the question. "Where do I want to be? In here, or out there?" The clever cow had made me seriously think about the answer. "Well, I'd like to be in here, with Mum and Cordelia, or, out there, with Mum and Cordelia."

She giggled and pulled me in for a motherly cuddle. "Silly, not having a proper answer. You've got to be somewhere, and once you've made up your mind, you've got to stay there. They're the rules, and we all have to live or die by the rules."

I stood up, abruptly, and glared at her. "I've got my own rules! You stick with yours, I'll stick with mine." I stamped my foot, but never went up to my room, just stared hard into her plain face, then calmly I asked, "So, who makes *your* rules? Hey?"

"I know what you're thinking, *Boss*, but you're wrong to think that. He has to live by the same rules, we all have to, even you, and whatever rules you think you live to, will turn out to be the same as ours. That's why you're here, to live with us as a happy family. I'm your sister, you're mine." She stood up and pulled me to her. "It's a good life once you get used to it, better than out there. And it's fate."

Fate? That's as bad as saying 'It's God's will', all a load of gypsy twaddle, and I wasn't about to start believing. I was just about ready to walk. All the confusion of the past few weeks had become even deeper, and I felt like I was being dragged in. Then, I wondered if Mary was helping me, or imprisoning me. I decided to find out.

"Right, you've convinced me! I either stay here with you lot, or go outside with that lot, and I can't have both, can I. Is that what you're saying, that I'm a prisoner if I stay? And you? Are you my cellmate, or prison warden? Well, answer me that. Cellmate, or prison warden?"

She looked down into her lap, and tried to ignore me. I sat down beside her and patiently waited for her to answer. Eventually she looked at me, smiling. "I'm neither. I'm like your big sister, and I'll miss you when you're gone. Really. But never mind, you'll be back."

I kept forgetting that she could see the future, or, at least claim to be able. She knew that I was going, even before I did, but, as she had said previously, nobody really wants to know their future, so she won't tell it, because nobody would choose their real future, just their dreams. She had something that she didn't want to tell me about mine.

"Well, Sis, you know I've got to go. I'm going down to Blythburgh, to find my other family, and bring them back here, unless I can get hold of Joshua, somehow. He's got James."

She shook her head, but smiled. "Perhaps he has, we never found his body. Never give up on your dreams, but never lose sight of reality. You know the rest."

"Joshua told me that."

"I know." She studied my face before, "I won't tell you your future, but, one day, maybe I'll read your palm and tell you your past. If you want to know it."

CHAPTER 27
GOING SOUTH

Luke and Three were busy taking barrels into the servery, and humping them up onto the bench, while Mary scrubbed her tables, so, I went to my room and retrieved the sovereigns from the floor. I also rolled up a blanket with my thick woollen shawl, put on my strongest shoes over thick socks, then tied the shawl, blanket and some personals into a tight bundle, ready for the long journey. I was leaving for the south.

Suddenly, I felt panic seeping into my whole body, and I shook. Was I really leaving? Why? I had a loyal new family who seem to want for nothing, and I'm warm, safe and well fed, so, why am I leaving? Am I ever to come back? But, then I remembered why I was leaving such a privileged new life: Mum and Cordelia.

Then, what about James? I saw something near the river, and was convinced that it was James with Joshua, so he could be here, looking for me, or he could have gone back to Devon with Joshua and be safe. Why me? What have I done to deserve such dilemmas? I've always been a good girl, worked hard and helped others, especially James and Cordelia, so why is God setting me these impossible challenges: James, or Mum and Cordelia? I sank onto the wooden floor and sobbed.

Eventually, I went downstairs, to talk to Mary about it.

"Please don't tell Luke, but I'm going to get Mum and Cordelia, and bring them back here. Whatever Luke thinks about it, I'm going. If I get back, it'll be up to Luke, it's his pub. Have to lodge elsewhere if he's not agreeable."

She took hold of my hand. "I know you're going, so I've packed some dried pork and beans and made you up a skin of boiled water. You mustn't drink the water on the road, they've had blisters and shits down in Wrentham. So, I'll see you when you get back."

How did she know all this? "You're just a pikie at heart, Madame Mary."

We had a cuddle, before she warned me, "Don't forget what I told you, they can't come back here, yet. So, see you in a few years. And I ain't goin' to tell you when that is, so go, before you change your mind." She looked into my face, then stroked my forrid. "And don't think like that, James is safe, and you can't bring him back here, anyway, so, while you're away I'll look out for James. Might be able to get a message to him, if he's a good little boy and behaving himself, so, go."

She let go of my hand.

"But Mary, what if Luke won't let them come here?"

"Don't worry about that, Boss is just his nickname." She gave me a wink, then pushed me towards the door. "Get out, sooner you go, sooner you'll be back, Sister."

Why was I going? And why wouldn't she tell what she knows, we trust each other. But as I was walking through the door and wondering, I remembered a previous conversation, when she mentioned the rules. I tried to forget it all as I set out on the long walk to Blythburgh. I expected it to take four or five days, more than enough thinking time, so I thought about the current situation, my route.

As I approached the bridge, I could see a familiar face on the opposite bank, that of Sampson Heron, the krooli who thought that he had purchased me. I couldn't go over while he was there, so I put my head down and went downriver to the ferry. When I approached the landing stage, I felt my tummy to make sure the money bag was still there, and held on tight to my tiny fortune and meagre belongings. The ferry was dropping people off on the opposite bank. I had to wait.

About ten minutes later, as the ferry approached our side, a big hand lumped onto my shoulder, and I jumped.

"Talk to me, please."

It was Luke.

I huffed, "Did Mary tell you?"

"Of course not, but if she had, it would've been for the right reasons. We all love you, so, stay with us." He pulled me into his big chest. "Don't go, please."

I looked up into his face, and I saw what I saw when he pulled me out of the river, a very concerned, round, fat, red face. It was as if I was going back into the river, leaving all this behind, perhaps for ever.

"You can bring them back here, when the time's right, they'll always be welcome. But you can't do it for a long time yet. Please wait until the time, then we can all get them, please, you can't get them yet, and you may never come back if you go alone. Please stay. Please."

His begging was genuine, I could tell.

"Why? Why can't they come back now?"

"They can't." He closed his eyes. "Stay here with us, and Mary'll look after you, until Mum and Cordelia are right, and then you can have all your family here, even James, one day. There's room for all of us, one big, happy family."

I had tears in my eyes, and he noticed.

"You mustn't cry over it, it's all good, but confusing, so don't cry, you've nothing to cry about. You'll all be together one day."

The ferryman was waiting for me, so I waved him to go back over with the other passengers. I would get the next one over.

"Am I safe here?"

"Of course, always, forever. We're all safe, this is the good World, and we're part of it. You're part of it, so please don't walk away from it all."

He wasn't the cuddliest, nor the most romantic man, but he had something which I was drawn to, and I didn't know what. It wasn't love, more like belonging, so I thought a bit about it as the ferry went over to the Yarmouth side.

"I saw the krooli at the bridge. Was he waiting for me?"

"Perhaps. But he can't hurt you, can't make you do anything, can't even kidnap you, so don't be afraid of him. Just look him in the face and smile. That's probably all he really wants, to be liked, poor old cunt. But that's another story, for another day, so, stay and I can tell you loads of stories, about all sorts of people. I've seen them all."

It wasn't making total sense, as there was always something absent from our conversations, and I began to wonder if it was the truth which was missing. How could three people be so good? It didn't add up in a World of dogged survival, where man eats man and dog eats dog. Why were they so good? I thought of Joshua, and I knew that he could explain if only he was here, and I knew that, as man of the cloth, he would *never* tell me that it was God's will. We'd already been down that route.

"I've got to try to get them back here. Please let me go."

He shook his smiling head. "I can't stop you, nobody can, only you. So, when you can, bring them back here, and I promise we'll all be happy, until the seas turn red."

I didn't know what that meant, either, so I kissed him on the cheek and turned towards the ferry, which was unloading the other side. I twisted round to say goodbye and thank you, but Luke was gone.

Well, this was it, leaving officially, for better or for worse, and I tried to put the strange words of wisdom which both Mary and Luke and given me, well out of my mind. I also tried to stop thinking about the missing bits, those little mysteries, which Mary couldn't or wouldn't explain.

I smiled up at the warm sun. It was perfect weather for travelling, especially as I was to sleep rough for the next four nights. I was tempted to say a short, silent prayer.

CHAPTER 28
HEAVEN AND BACK AGAIN

As I stood watching the ferryman disembark his three passengers I started to get the butterflies, so, I sat down on the stage to wait. Then the ferryman waved to me, indicating that he was stopping for his dinner, leaving me stranded on the Vauxhall side of the Bure. I dozed off.

I don't know how long I had been dozing for, but when I awoke, the ferry was just leaving the opposite bank. I couldn't believe it. I had to rub my eyes and look again, and make suer that I was awake.

"James! James, it's you!"

I jumped up and panted as I waited for the ferry, which was carrying two passengers, James and Joshua. My head swooned as they approached.

"James! Joshua. It's really you, my family." I screamed as the ferry touched the staging, and Joshua looked at me as if he'd never seen me before. "It's me, Eunice!"

I grabbed James as he stepped onto the staging, and he cried.

"But...." He stood in my arms, and studied my face. "It's really you." His head pulled into my breast, just like the old days, when he was worrying. "But you're...." He just snivelled into my breasts, and I felt I had gone to heaven and back again. Then I looked to Joshua. He didn't even acknowledge me, just put his hand onto James's shoulder.

"I'll go and see if they're taking passengers on the next train. You wait here with your friend, but don't leave this landing. Promise?"

James nodded his answer.

Once Joshua had gone, I asked, "Where have you been? I've searched for you, and so has everyone else, but never found you. And here you are." I still couldn't believe it.

"Where've you been?"

He pulled out from my smothering hug. "I've been at home, with Lanky. Where else would I go? But, where've you been? I thought...."

What had he thought? He wasn't even pleased to see me. What's happening?

I was careful with my answer. "I've been with Luke and Three, and Mary. You'll love them, and they'll love you."

"Who're they?"

"They live in The Vauxhall Room. The pub. Just down there, near the bridge." I pointed that way. "Shall we go there?"

"I can't. Uncle Joshua told me not to go anywhere. He's taking me to Dorchester, where his church is." He still looked me in the face, questioning my thoughts, like he used to when we were kicked out of the house, when he was stressing.

"We're together again. Please come with me, or, I could come to Dorchester. I've got money."

"But you can't. How can you?"

"Easy." Then I thought of Mum and Cordelia. "You're right, I can't yet. I'll go down and get Mum and Cordelia out, then we can all come to Dorchester. The family together again. Like heaven."

But he wasn't really taking it in, or he didn't want to know, he just stared into my eyes to read my thoughts. Eventually, his eyes became wet. He whimpered, "Do you remember what happened on the bridge?"

I nodded. "Some of it. I thought I'd killed you, let you go to save myself. How are you still here? No, don't answer that, you're here, and we don't want to know why. We can just look at the future, forget the past."

"I can't forget it. I've tried, but I can't." His little eight-year-old face frowned like an old one. "I can't forget. I can't forgive myself for what I did. I'm sorry, Eunice, I love you." He pulled in for a cry.

I couldn't cry with him, I was too happy, so I gently rocked him in my arms as he cried for both of us. Then, I could see Joshua coming back from the train terminal. He was just a couple of minutes away.

I had to talk, we were running out of time. "You mustn't blame yourself, it was all an accident. I spent ages blaming myself for letting you go, nightmares, horrible nightmares, but Mary has always told me not to stress over it. You'll love Mary, she's a Romany palm-reader, sort of." I had a giggle, but he didn't.

He just looked into my face, and very quietly suggested, "Don't listen to her. Dad always said they were liars and cheats, so, don't believe a word of it." He continued to study my face. "I'm sorry, I didn't mean to let go. I couldn't hold on any longer." He snivelled. "I've got to go with Uncle Joshua, soon."

I began to sink. He didn't want me, so he *must* blame me. That's why he's so cold towards me.

"Look, Joshua's nearly here, so go with him, he'll look after you, and when I've got Mum and Cordelia out, we'll come to Dorchester, and be together again." I looked at Joshua approaching, who never even seemed to know who I was. "I love you, and don't blame yourself for anything. Promise me. Now, go to Joshua, and I'll go to Mum and Cordelia. Love you forever."

His face was still cold, and the only emotions seemed to be confusion and regret.

"Why're you going to Blythburgh?"

"I told you, to get Mum and Cordelia, because I have some money that should have been Dad's.... well it's a long story. But that's why I'm going to Blythburgh, to get Mum and Cordelia."

"But Lanky said that I should go with Uncle Joshua, because he was moving to a new parish. He couldn't take me. So, I can't be with him, and I can't be with you. I can't."

Joshua was almost upon us.

"Lanky doesn't know what he's on about, he's a drunken junky. He hasn't gone to another parish, he's going to...." I just couldn't say it to James. "He was a good man, but lost his head."

"That's not true. He would have kept me there, if he could, I know it."

I nodded in agreement. Perhaps he didn't need to know the know the truth, why would he? So, I suggested, "You go off with Joshua, and I'll go to Mum, and we'll all see you soon."

"Don't be stupid!" He pushed away from me and scowled, before running towards Joshua, but stopped halfway and turned to me. "You can't get them out! How can you, when you're dead?"

Next thing I remember is looking up at the ferryman's bearded face, as he shook me to wake up. He was smiling.

I sweated, as the he gently helped me to my feet and suggested, "Go home to Luke. They're all waiting for you. Your family."

"Has James gone?"

"The boy? He's gone off with that vicar. Gone back, where you can't go, so go home to Luke, Mary and Three. They're expecting you." He turned back to his ferry.

I asked him politely, "Do you know Luke well, Sir?"

"Yes, very well. We were in Canton together, but we weren't no more use to the navy, dead."

CHAPTER 29
OH WELL

As the the weight of confusion slowly lifted from my shoulders, I wandered back along the river to The Vauxhall Room. It was, is, my home, and always will be. I felt like I was in an open prison, not locked up, but not allowed out.

"Here, this'll help." Mary sat with me in front of the fire, and handed me a shot of whisky. "They say that drinking whisky will kill you. That's what they say in the rows, but not here, not this side. Drink as much as you want."

I was slowly beginning to understand what had been missing from conversation all this time. It seems that the rules don't allow us to talk about it openly, the fact that we're all dead. Even Luke and Three never talked about it. 'If you can't save the others, save yourself. You're no use to the navy dead.' Luke disobeyed his naval instinct, and went back for Three and the 'Ferryman'. He chose to die, trying to save them. Yes, Luke Smith is a fine man, and I'll give him my hand, but it won't be for life, it'll be for death.

Mary once told me that she wouldn't tell me my future, but one day she would tell me my past, and I believe that on that very night, she did. In her own mysterious way, she explained.

I had gone to sleep, then the dreams all started up, and she showed me my past. As James was pulled out of the water, he desperately hung onto my hand, but it slipped out, and I went down to my watery grave. I came to this world, and James stayed in his.

When I asked Mary why she had never explained it all to me earlier, she emphasized that it was against the rules, and besides, "You would never have believed a word of it."

Maybe not, but what about these rules that they all go on about? "And what about these rules? Whose rules, Boss's"

"Don't be silly that's just his nickname, goes with his job. His job is Boss, and Three's job is tender and bouncer."

"And me? Do I have a job?"

She thought carefully about that one. "If you're staying, you'll have to work. Yes, I'll give you the job of Peter Fuller's Daughter. You're good at that one, the good the bad and the very pretty, and I'd say you've passed the probationary period with flying colours. Yes, that'll do you fine, and it'll add a bit of variety to our lives, right here in Vauxhall."

As I tell my own story, I'm still not sure if I believe a word of it, but Mary tells me that it's all true, cross her gypsy heart.

So, right here in The Vauxhall Room, we all ~~lived~~ existed happily forever after.

The end.